"You are mine now," the man said, but Alinta didn't understand his utterings. She had never heard this language before, and to her it was gibberish. The look in his eye though, that was universal. She had seen such looks at the gatherings. Her father and mother had both worked hard to keep the men away from her at these events, but she didn't believe anyone could save her this time. She thought she could see what he wanted in his look, and when he grabbed her arm, she knew she wasn't wrong.

The thought of him touching her was repugnant. He smelled so unlike the men she had grown up with and expected to one day belong to. His sweat was sharp and foreign, and the white of his skin was different from anything she had ever known. She looked around and the leers on the faces of the other men told their tale. They knew what Bradley had in mind for her. There was no hope for it. Alinta resigned herself to whatever the fates had decided for her.

A K'Anne Meinel novella

Also by K'Anne Meinel:

Novels in Paperback:

SHIPS *CompanionSHIP, FriendSHIP,*
RelationSHIP
Long Distance Romance
Children of Another Mother
Erotica
The Claim
Bikini's Are Dangerous
The Complete Series
Germanic
Malice Masterpieces 1
The First Five Books
Represented
Timed Romance
Malice Masterpieces 2
Books Six through Ten
The Journey Home
Out at the Inn
Shorts
Anthology Volume 1
Lawyered
Malice Masterpieces 3
Books Eleven through Fifteen
Blown Away

Blown Away
The Alternate Cover
Small Town Angel
Pirated Love
Doctored
Veil of Silence
Malice Masterpieces 4
Books Sixteen through Twenty
The Outsider
Pirated Heart
Recombinant Love
Survivors
Inn the Dog House
Flight
An Island Between Us

Vetted Series:
Vetted
Cavalcade (Prequel)
Pioneering (Prequel)
Vetted Further
Vetted Again

Novellas in Paperback:

Mysterious Malice (Book 1)
Meticulous Malice (Book 2)
Mistaken Malice (Book 3)
Malicious Malice (Book 4)
Masterful Malice (Book 5)
Matrimonial Malice (Book 6)
Mourning Malice (Book 7)
Murderous Malice (Book 8)
Mental Malice (Book 9)
Menacing Malice (Book 10)
Minor Malice (Book 11)
Morally Malice (Book 12)
Morose Malice (Book 13)
Melancholy Malice (Book 14)
Mad Malice (Book 15)
Macabre Malice (Book 16)

Marinating Malice (Book 17)
Macerating Malice (Book 18)
Minacious Malice (Book 19)
Meddlesome Malice (Book 20)
Meandering Malice (Book 21)
Vaquera Safica (Spanish)
Surfista Safica (Spanish)
ケーアンヌ・マイネル (Japanese)
Maniacal Malice (Book 22)
Sayyida
The Northwood Lodge
Monitoring Malice (Book 23)
Marked Malice (Book 24)
Shanghaied

Pocket Paperbacks:

Mysterious Malice (Book 1)
Sapphic Surfer
Sapphic Cowgirl
Meticulous Malice (Book 2)
Mistaken Malice (Book 3)
Malicious Malice (Book 4)
Masterful Malice (Book 5)
Matrimonial Malice (Book 6)
Mourning Malice (Book 7)
Murderous Malice (Book 8)

Mental Malice (Book 9)
Menacing Malice (Book 10)
Minor Malice (Book 11)
Morally Malice (Book 12)
Morose Malice (Book 13)
Melancholy Malice (Book 14)
Mad Malice (Book 15)
Macabre Malice (Book 16)
Marinating Malice (Book 17)

In E-Book Format:
Short Stories

Fantasy
Wet & Wet Again
Family Night
Quickie ~ Against the Car
Quickie ~ Against the Wall
Quickie ~ Over the Couch
Mile High Club
Quickie ~ Under the Pier
Heel or Heal
Kiss
Family Night 2
Beach Dreams
Internet Dreamers
Snoggered

On the Parkway
Stable Affair
Kept
Stolen
Agitated
Love of my LIFE
Quickie in an Elevator,
GOING DOWN?
Into the Garden
The Book Case
The Other Women
Menage a WHAT?

E-Book Novellas

Children of Another Mother
Bikini's are Dangerous
Ghostly Love
Bikini's are Dangerous 2
Sapphic Surfer
The Rockhound
Bikini's are Dangerous 3
Bikini's are Dangerous 4
Bikini's are Dangerous 5
Mysterious Malice (Book 1)
Meticulous Malice (Book 2)
Mistaken Malice (Book 3)
Malicious Malice (Book 4)
Masterful Malice (Book 5)
Matrimonial Malice (Book 6)
Mourning Malice (Book 7)
Murderous Malice (Book 8)
Sapphic Cowgirl
Sapphic Cowboi
Mental Malice (Book 9)
Menacing Malice (Book 10)

Charming Thief
~Snake Island~
Charming Thief
~Diamonds are a Girls Best Friend~
Minor Malice (Book 11)
Morally Malice (Book 12)
Morose Malice (Book 13)
Melancholy Malice (Book 14)
Mad Malice (Book 15)
Macabre Malice (Book 16)
Marinating Malice (Book 17)
Macerating Malice (Book 18)
Minacious Malice (Book 19)
Sayyida
Meddlesome Malice (Book 20)
Meandering Malice (Book 21)
Maniacal Malice (Book 22)
The Northwood Lodge
Monitoring Malice (Book 23)
Marked Malice (Book 24)

E-Book Novels

SHIPS *CompanionSHIP, FriendSHIP,*
RelationSHIP
Erotica Volume 1
Long Distance Romance
Bikini's Are Dangerous
The Complete Series
Malice Masterpieces
The First Five Books
To Love a Shooting Star
Germanic
The Claim
Represented
Timed Romance
Blown Away
Blown Away *The Alternate Cover*
Malice Masterpieces 2
Books Six through Ten
The Journey Home
Out at the Inn
Anthology Volume 1
Lawyered

Malice Masterpieces 3
Books Eleven through Fifteen
Small Town Angel
Pirated Love
Doctored
Veil of Silence
Malice Masterpieces 4
Books Sixteen through Twenty
The Outsider
Pirated Heart
Recombinant Love
Survivors
Inn the Dog House
Flight
An Island Between Us

Vetted Series:
Vetted
Cavalcade (Prequel)
Pioneering (Prequel)
Vetted Further
Vetted Again

LARGE Print Novels

SHIPS CompanionSHIP, FriendSHIP,
RelationSHIP
Erotica Volume 1
Long Distance Romance
Children of Another Mother
Bikini's Are Dangerous
The Complete Series

Malice Masterpieces
The First Five Books
To Love a Shooting Star
The Claim
Represented
Timed Romance

Audiobooks

Doctored
Sapphic Surfer
The Rockhound
Cavalcade

Pioneering
To Love A Shooting Star
Mysterious Malice

Videos

Biography of Books
Ships
Sapphic Surfer
Ghostly Love
Long Distance Romance
Germanic
Sensual Sapphic
Sapphic Cowgirl
Couples
Lie Next To Me

Sapphic Cowboi
Timed Romance
Readings (SHIPS)
Doctored
Veil of Silence
She's Coming (The Outsider short)
It's Coming (The Outsider short)
The Outsider
Vetted

K'ANNE MEINEL

OUTBACK BORN

ISBN-13: 978-1733661140

Copyright © August 2019 by K'Anne Meinel

K'Anne Meinel is available for comments at KAnneMeinel@aim.com as well as on Facebook @ http://www.facebook.com/K.Anne.Meinel.Fan.Page, Google + @ https://plus.google.com/u/2/+KAnneMeinel, LinkedIn @ https://www.linkedin.com/in/k-anne-meinel-a026385a, or her blog @ http://kannemeinel.wordpress.com/ or on Twitter @ https://twitter.com/KAnneMeinel, or on her website @ www.kannemeinel.com if you would like to follow her to find out about stories and book's releases.

www.shadoepublishing.com

ShadoePublishing@gmail.com

Shadoe Publishing, LLC is a United States of America company

Cover by: K'Anne Meinel @ Shadoe Publishing
Edited by: Deb Amia, Grammar Queen grammarqueen.com

**Dedicated to anyone who
thinks I'm writing about them.
I am.**

PUBLISHER'S NOTE

This is a work of fiction. Names, characters, places, and incidents are the product of the author's imagination or are used fictitiously, and any resemblance to actual persons, living or dead, business establishments, events, or locales is entirely coincidental.

The publisher does not have any control over and does not assume any responsibility for author or third-party Web sites or their content.

CHAPTER ONE

The heat would have killed a lesser man or woman, but the small group was used to it. They stood there for a moment, each standing on one leg as they waited. Had they sat on the ground or laid down; the heat would have been infinitely worse. The sand was blistering hot to the touch. By standing with only one foot touching the scorching sands at a time, it lessened the amount of fiery heat their bodies had to deal with. The woman and girl watched warily as the male leader chewed thoughtfully before pointing with his chin, grunting out a command, and nodding. A young boy rushed up, just in time for them all to head out again. Resentfully, he sighed at the missed opportunity for a rest. The older man glared warningly at him for a moment, and when the young boy glanced over, he saw a similar look on the older woman and an almost smug look on the young girl's face. She turned and headed out, following the older man, who had immediately turned away.

Moving around a spinifex, the boy startled two lizards sheltering in its welcoming and limited shade. His spear caught one, and he sliced it open neatly, bringing it to his mouth immediately and enjoying the still warm blood, which dripped down his chin as he ate. He rapidly walked on, trying to catch up to the older man but keeping far enough away that he could hunt and protect them.

The older woman, his dam, scooped up the second lizard and crushed its head before she stuffed it in the woven bag slung around her shoulders. The lizard's tail twitched as it was in the throes of dying. She too noticed the heat but in an absent way, the thick soles of her feet protecting her from its burn as the heat reflected off the red sands. Her eyes traveled around the spinifex, hoping for another lizard and annoyed that her son had been such a glutton and eaten the first. Her eyes scanned the area, looking for other targets, her resentment fading as she began walking rapidly towards where her family had already disappeared.

They spread out attempting to scavenge as much as possible in this sparse and bare territory, out of sight of each other but within hearing distance. The young girl gathered items as she traveled her own path. She looked about the area, not fearful of its enormous expanse. She was unable to see her family but was not afraid since she knew generally where they might be. The family had spread out to hunt and scavenge while traveling over the vast terrain. They were one with their environment, specially adapted to an area not intended to support many, and yet, many lived here, far flung over hundreds of miles. Occasionally, she lifted her head, able to scent her family on the faint

breeze. She knew the difference between the scent of prey, the smell of fear, and the common body odors that identified her family.

Alinta heard a sound, and she immediately crouched at the noise, understanding the unique piercing sound, almost like a whistle, was a signal from her sire warning of danger. She held her own woven gathering bag tightly to her side, a carved stick held in a protective pose should she need to defend herself or she was called to defend the family. She balanced the water urn, a small bark vessel, on her head, keeping her neck straight and stiff, so it didn't fall off. Alinta tested the air, smelling for the source of potential danger. She heard the clicking sound of her dam trying to locate her children. Alinta clicked back. It was short and sweet but delivered in a way that carried on the still air of the desert. She heard a nearly identical sound from her brother at almost the same moment but coming from a different direction. She knew better than to make any other noise, which might give away their location to the danger that held them frozen in the underbrush, possibly scaring off necessary game. After a while, she heard her father make another whistling sound, releasing them from the command to stay hidden and silent while danger was about. Not knowing the source of the danger, Alinta headed out again in the same direction, this time, her senses were heightened, and while she scavenged, she was on high alert for the danger her father had sensed, although she knew she might never know what he had sensed or seen. After all, he certainly wouldn't discuss it with her, a mere girl.

The hours passed as they traveled in a northeasterly direction using ancient paths that only they could see. They avoided traveling on the path itself, instead remaining nearby in order to hunt and gather. Some of these paths were called song trails, named by the elders who understood such things. The people accepted this information without questioning their superior knowledge. The mysticism of these trails was knowledge only given to the elders, and it was passed down from generation to generation.

Alinta found grubs and other insects, which she stuffed in her mouth as she traveled. This was permissible as she hunted for bigger game such as lizards, snakes, and rodents. She also gathered a bundle of sticks, slowly building a pile under one arm while keeping the other hand and arm free to poke and prod and defend with her stick if necessary. Late in the day, her father managed to stun and then kill a small kangaroo, and they stopped for the day to cook the abundance of meat. He chose a small gully where he could look out on the higher bank. He waited for his son and indicated he was to take another position across the gully on another bank.

Alinta's mother pulled out pieces of fluff she had gathered from small nests and some flint she would use to draw a spark. With a quick and practiced movement, she drew the flint against another stone. She leaned down to blow on the spark that landed in her tinder, puffing gently until the spark turned into a flame. Slowly, she added bits and pieces of smaller twigs and later, some of the wood they had gathered. Finally, they had a small fire to cook their game. Alinta and her mother ran the pelt of the kangaroo across the flame, singeing off the hair. The smell was terrible, but they were accustomed to it and were able to ignore it. None of them would eat the pelt of the animal. Then, her mother raked the coals into a small hole she had dug, and they placed the kangaroo in the hole, piling on more wood, grasses, and leaves, so it would cook thoroughly. As the hours passed, the delicious smell of cooked meat filled the air, dissipating any leftover smell of burnt hair,

and finally, her father came down from his guard position on the bank. Her mother pulled back the coals, twigs, burnt grasses, and leaves to reveal the juicy, cooked meat. Alinta tried not to resent her father's gluttony as he ate first, her mother's warning glance cutting off any sign of resentment as Alinta opened her gathering bag, reached in, and began to gnaw on a lizard she pulled out. Her mother contributed more grubs and a snake, and between them they ate. Her brother twitched impatiently from where he still stood watch on the ridge, the aroma of the cooked meat making him hungry. He eventually switched places with his sire and ate to his heart's content, casting superior looks towards his sister before returning to guard the family.

At a signal from her sire, Alinta's mother cut out a piece of the meat for the two of them using a stone that had been sharpened and chipped on one side. The other side fit in her palm and allowed her to manage the stone. The sizzling of the fat on the coals was loud in the still evening as the fire died down and they ate. Both women wanted to eat more, but Alinta's mother covered the meat, saving some for the next day. The small kangaroo wouldn't last long between two hungry males and two starving females.

The family continued their scavenging in the coming days, only heading back south in their eternal quest to find food and survive on the sparse land when the weather began to change and become colder. Alinta shivered at night, grateful when her mother joined her to share body heat. Her mother was sometimes called to duty, servicing her husband as he attempted to get more children from her aging body. Alinta wondered at this. Her father's rutting seemed to give him pleasure, but her mother's resigned and vacant looks told the young girl

she wasn't enjoying the deed, and her brother's amused look confused her.

Alinta didn't understand when her body had begun to change this season. No longer was her body straight and flat. Her flow had come to her, and her breasts had grown. Now, she ached monthly. Her hips were also rounding, and she had become taller. Her mother explained about keeping herself clean and answering a husband's needs when the time came for her to be given to the proper man. She also explained about how to entice a man into becoming aroused. Alinta didn't enjoy these instructions, finding them embarrassing, and she was relieved when her mother stopped. She was more interested in the plants her mother showed her that helped to relieve the aches and pains her body suffered during her monthly flow.

Her father headed for their ancestral gathering grounds, the bora grounds, signs of other families and other people becoming more obvious as they came closer to the sacred area. A broken twig and a dislodged stone told their tales of others in the vicinity. Her father and brother moved in closer to protect her mother and sister, keeping them constantly in view as they came closer to others. Alinta knew this was because other roving bands of people frequently looked for and captured women for wives. Her mother, while no longer in her prime, could still bear children, so she had value. Alinta, since becoming a woman and having her first flow, was now extremely valuable. Her father grunted out a command to her mother, and Alinta now wore a flap of the kangaroo pelt across her middle, hiding her charms from any who might see her. At night, her father slept closer to them, his spear held in his hand, ready to charge up and defend his daughter, his most valuable asset.

Alinta had been raised in a harsh environment. The desert winds burnished and toughened her skin to the color of dark honey. Centuries of breeding ensured that her skin was darker than some tribes but lighter than others. Her mother's people, lighter than her father's, instilled a cast to her skin that others did not have. Her features were a delicate blend of her parents'. Her nose was finer, and her face was narrower than most in her tribe. Her girlish figure was taking on a woman's curves as her menses changed her from a mere girl into a woman. Her mother spent a great deal of time explaining about taking care of herself during this important time—how to please her mate, how to be a helpful wife, and what duties were expected of her. Alinta simply accepted this as she knew no better, but a tiny curl of resentment grew within her over the freedoms enjoyed by her brother. He was not watched as closely, and he was able to come and go at will, answerable only to their father, who ruled them all with an iron hand. Alinta was pleased when her mother once again finished explaining her duties. She found them uncomfortable to discuss, and when asked, she had no further questions for her mother. She would accept her fate when she was given to the man her father would eventually choose.

The land seemed to become more arid as they headed to the bora grounds. Finding water was becoming more difficult, but the aboriginal people knew their land and the strata where water flowed below the desert sands. When they needed to fill their water urns, they would stop near the rocks in a place familiar to Alinta's mother, and she would begin to dig using a coolamon, a shallow vessel her mother had pecked out of stone in order to dig in the desert sands. Alinta helped her, pushing the sand away from the hole she was digging. Slowly, inch by inch, foot by foot, she dug down into the hard-packed

sands, throwing the sand up on the sides while Alinta pulled it back carefully from the edge. Finally, she began handing up full vessels of sand, which slowly became damp, and Alinta dumped them well away from the hole her mother was in. She handed the coolamon back frequently as they continued to dig. Eventually, they found a bit of bark her mother had buried there previously, and below this they found cool, refreshing water. She handed down her water urn, and her mother sloshed the water in it until it was full. Alinta took a drink of this cool water before handing down her mother's urn and listening to her fill it. The air of the desert felt cool against her bare skin, the damp sands giving off no heat as the sun set. She carefully put the urns to the side, woven leaves covering their tops to prevent evaporation. Alinta then handed the bark to her mother, who cautiously covered the hole once again and began to push sand back on it to prevent evaporation. Slowly, her mother's head rose from the hole as she stomped the dirt back in place, and Alinta helped her hide the water hole. Together they wiped away all signs of their digging, hiding their source of water from any casual observers.

They quickly took their urns to the campsite Alinta's father had chosen. Alinta handed her father her urn, bowing her head as he took a drink. Her mother offered the same to her son, cutting him off when he would have drunk more than his fair share. Her mother soon had a small fire going where they cooked the mice, lizards, and snakes they had caught that day. The offerings were few and were supplemented with desert fruit, quandongs, and seeds, small things that meant the difference between life and death to the people who lived in this arid region of Australia.

CHAPTER TWO

The gathering was about one hundred people, but it made up of a lot of people who broke off into solitary families that contained only six to ten people at most. Smaller groups were a necessity since this land couldn't support a large population. Centuries of breeding and culture and solitary wanderings meant they could survive in this arid region. The people came together to exchange stories, swap goods, and trade for wives. Alinta shook with fear as the men and older boys assessed her, looking at her now growing breasts, her height, and her womanly hips. Her mother had been a good breeder, giving her husband four children and only two had died. She was still young enough to give him more offspring, and they speculated amongst themselves if Alinta would be as prolific or as good a wife. That they spoke of this in front of Alinta as she passed and was within hearing, showed how little they cared for her feelings on the matter. Alinta was terrified her father would trade her for things he needed or wanted. She didn't want to leave her mother, and yet, she knew she would have no choice in the matter. Eventually, her father would find a man that he wanted something from, and she would be turned over.

While the women sat and gossiped, the men went off to do the mysterious things the women weren't privy to. The elders—older men of indeterminate years who held all the secrets of their tribe—went to the sacred grounds of their gathering, the bora circle, and into huts that had been built before any could remember. They performed secret, sacred rituals only they knew, painting themselves and a few chosen men with esoteric symbols and holding meetings. The women supplied them with cooked food, bringing it to a chosen spot and setting it down, going no further into the men's areas as they were not interested in their secrets or rituals. Men would eventually return to their families, but for now, many stayed in the wurlies built at the site, sharing tales, women, or trade.

One of the men had come from a place far to the south and was telling terrific tales of men of lighter skin, who rode odd animals and killed from afar with thunder and lightning. He had a rapt audience in the men and even some of the women that were near enough to hear but pretended they weren't listening avidly. Of more importance were the spearheads he had obtained; made of a stone no one had ever seen. It was almost perpetually sharp, not like the stones that chipped when the men used them to hunt. When he showed the others an axe made entirely of this new type of stone, greed and envy of his apparent wealth was obvious on every man's face.

The men must hunt, and this trader was able to show them the value of this new stone. The stone was lighter and more resilient. He could throw it farther, which meant he could escape easier if danger presented itself. He needn't worry about smashing a hard-earned and carefully crafted spear, and the *stone* seemed unbreakable and could be sharpened against other stones. The greed the other men felt over this newfound stone was discussed avidly at the gathering, and news of anything out of the ordinary they had found in their wanderings of their territory was shared.

Alinta examined the ancient, round, conical hut structures that were woven of brush. Few stayed in these huts, mostly the older, wise men, and they seemed to spend a lot of time doing spiritual things the young woman didn't understand. The young boys, some on the cusp of manhood, watched the girls and young women, imitating the men and watching enviously as other young men were included with the adults and elders. Alinta compared herself to other girls her age and made tentative overtures of friendship, although each was shy in her own way. She watched avidly as the men brought out didgeridoos, long, hollow tubes of various lengths, and other sound-making instruments. They were creating hauntingly beautiful music, and she saw where women and men both danced to the notes.

Women gossiped, compared babies, and talked about each other's children. It was one of the only times they gathered in a group large enough and social enough that they could do this, and it wouldn't be repeated until next year. Food and different plants were discussed, so every woman and girl would be able to identify these food sources should they find themselves in an unfamiliar area away from their home.

The gathering lasted four days. The men and boys competed to see who could throw a spear the farthest and the most accurately or who could fling a boomerang and make it return. The musicians of the tribe used their didgeridoos and rhythm sticks as the people built up to a corroberee, a party or celebration. Some of these instruments were older than the people using them, having been handed down from their elders, who imparted the magic and knowledge from within. Others were taught how to make these instruments, using ancient magic to pass on to the next generation these skills of creating the instruments and the magic of the music.

As the gathering broke up, Alinta's family headed farther south, not north to their accustomed area as they had expected. The surprise among the family members was obvious, but they dared not question her father, Omeo, who set out determinedly in this direction. They had traveled this way before but not in many years. It was part of their tribe's territory, but only certain families roamed this area. Alinta's family was usually farther north and west. It gave them an opportunity to explore and refamiliarize themselves with the ancient paths in this area. Alinta vaguely remembered being here before in her short life, and her brother was even more interested as this would show him new hunting grounds and teach him other paths that he too might follow someday.

As they headed south and east, the land changed. The spinifex grew longer, and both Alinta and her mother delightedly gathered the longer fronds and spent their evenings making new and stronger gathering bags that would replace their old ones when they wore out. The landscape seemed greener and lusher, and appeared to have more offerings. Hunting seemed marginally easier than in their normal

sparse areas too. The season had changed. Winter storms were bringing sudden and fierce rainstorms, which were washing away the buildup of oils, sweat, and dust on their skin, which felt odd. Their skin felt softer, smoother, and more vulnerable to the constant bugs that existed in their environment. If they spotted a storm quick enough and shelter was available, they would wait out the squall in the relative comfort of an overhang, looking curiously at the designs left by others, who had come before. Some were quite intricate, but others were faded and oblique. There must have been some way for them to draw so high, or, as her mother told a fascinated Alinta and her brother, older peoples must have been giants. They looked at the drawings they discovered on their travels with respect, awe, and trepidation, assigning them mysterious and mythical meanings they couldn't comprehend. At times when they camped in these places, their fire cast eerie shadows on the high rocks, making it appear that spirits moved among them, and they could feel the difference in the air around them.

They went on this way for many weeks, cautiously exploring new lands, traveling well beyond anywhere they had traveled before and well beyond their tribal grounds. The game was becoming more prevalent. Nightly, they had fresh meat, an unheard-of occurrence for these scavengers. They had to leave some of it behind, some of it spoiled before they could eat it all, and still, Alinta's father was able to find fresh meat for them to eat. The plants enabled them to gather fresh fruits and vegetables, and their regular meals made them feel slower and gluttonous. Alinta and her family all had more flesh on their bones than ever before with the bounty before them. They couldn't gather it all. Their bags were constantly full and heavy, and with the hunting that both her brother and father did, the abundance seemed

overwhelming. As they waited out the winter storms, Alinta and her mother would take the many seeds they had gathered on their trek and grind them into flour, making little balls that they could bake in the fire and creating delicious biscuit-like offerings to add to the abundance of food they were finding and consuming.

The rains continued for weeks as Alinta's father searched for and found signs of other human habitation. Confronted by another group of wandering tribesmen he didn't know, Omeo made himself known. Using signs and an occasional word, he kept their meeting from becoming contentious as the other travelers stared curiously at the intruders on their lands. They were permitted to continue their travels in this new land. The rainy season passed, and the hot, dry desert soaked up any moisture that had fallen, hiding it well in its sands.

One day, Alinta's father clicked, low. It carried through the still, hot air of the desert, and they all froze, eyes darting about looking for the danger he had signaled as the family blended into the brush, hidden from sight. They had noticed for some time that dust was being kicked up by something traveling along. It didn't act like a dust storm rolling along the landscape, rather it seemed like something was kicking up the dust. It took a while, but finally, Alinta was able to see what was coming and had caused her father to signal. An unlikely sight stretched before them. What looked like a greatly widened path rolling across the plains contained some sort of animal she had never seen before. She couldn't figure out what they were, but they were huge compared to the largest kangaroo she had ever seen. The animal seemed to have four legs, a snout, longer hairs at points, and a tail made up of even longer hairs. Its back was long and on top of it sat what looked like a man but was unlike any man she had ever seen before. Compared to

her father, these men were very pale and were wearing too many pelts in the hot spring sun, and they appeared to be one with the grotesque animal. Watching them, she noticed that some of the animals were on their own and did not have these grotesque animal-man combinations, and she was able to discern that they were several different beings. She watched in awe as they stopped and one of these aberrations got off the strange animal. He walked around the animal just as her father did, lifting its legs, one by one, to examine its feet. Her eyes darted about, wondering if her father wanted the family to run, attack, or hunt. She couldn't hear with her heart hammering in her ears. She had never been this frightened before.

Another strange sight rolled out before them, many strange animals with what looked like men sitting on some sort of rolling thing with bundles piled on it. Then another similar contrivance appeared, and another, and then there were more than Alinta could count although the number matched the total fingers on both her hands. She didn't understand their purpose and gazed at everything in awe. She could now make out that there were many pale men on these contraptions and several of the odd animals were pulling them. The animals were separate from the contraptions, not a part of them, and they were using the animals to pull them. How unusual to make an animal work for them! The smell was decidedly foreign as it wafted towards them on the small breeze. The odor was strange, strong, musky, and not in the least appealing. She could tell from the scent that the animals could be eaten, but the men also had a strange odor about them.

Her father finally made a noise, a clicking sound that drew the family closer, and he signaled that they should stay in sight of each other, something they rarely did as they traveled since spreading out allowed them to scavenge and hunt more. The family began to follow what was a caravan of wagons, although they didn't know they were called that. When Alinta caught her mother's glance she could see the same puzzlement in the older woman's look. A bonus of following the noisy men and their animals was that the game was scared off their trail, and the Aborigines were far enough away that the smaller animals were driven towards them. Their gathering bags bulged with lizards, rodents, and snakes in addition to produce from this abundant land. There was so much choice of prey being driven towards them, they had a choice whether they would catch and kill or allow them to remain free.

When night came upon them, they made their camp far away from the white man's camp, and after eating his share of their catch, her father indicated they should stay where they were while he went off into the night. He studied the white man's camp for a long time before making his decision.

He appeared suddenly in the light of the white man's fire, causing several to grab their guns in consternation. He seemed unearthly at first, an apparition, startling some.

"What do you want?" someone finally asked him cautiously.

Omeo, Alinta's father, turned his head as though to try and understand these foreign words. He had been very brave to seek out these white men. He desired their *stones*, and he had seen several examples of the material in use around their camp. His eyes took in everything: the two types of large animals that they used as beasts of burden tied off to one side, some animals with ropes tied around their long legs, and the men sitting around the large fire…much larger than it needed to be. He was frightened but wanted to trade for the wonders he

had seen at the gathering, namely the stone axe that would not break and the stone that stayed sharp even if it was hit against a hard stump or broke a rib. This stone could be sharpened against other stones, so it was perfect for spear tips. It had been explained to him that only white men had this stone. That was why he had traveled into unfamiliar territory and risked running into strange tribes in order to seek out the white man. He had been aware of the dust in the air for several days, hoping it will lead him to find these men.

He had looked warily about their camp before approaching, only the horses aware of his presence as he blended in with the dark of the night. Several horses blew out their noses as they scented the nearly feral man. The oxen placidly chewed their cuds, occasionally flicking their long tails at the incessant bugs that plagued them all. Omeo had nearly run back into the night several times before making his presence known to the men. He was still ready to run if they displayed any aggression. He held his spear ready but in a fashion that might not be construed as threatening. He glanced at one of the men, who was dark enough and had features like their people, but Omeo wasn't certain he was one of them. Omeo made a gesture with his free hand, but no one saw it because of their reliance on verbal language.

It seemed it would be impossible to make his wishes known. He wished to trade for their stones, but they couldn't understand him. He tried again, and still, no one saw the gesture. He heard them speak, and the qualifying note at the end signified it was a question. He couldn't understand this language so unlike his own and the few languages he knew of other tribes. It was too melodic, had too much song in it from what he could tell. He couldn't understand the meaning, and he cocked his head.

"What do you think he wants?" one of the men asked another.

"Probably food," was the response as they watched the skinny Aborigine. From the way he was dressed—only a small pouch covering his genitals with a string leading around his bony hips to hold it up and nothing else—he looked like he hadn't eaten in a while. If he were able to tell them he had eaten more in the past few days of his life than he had in the many weeks prior, they would be surprised.

Omeo had an idea. This was something that wouldn't be necessary in his own tribe where he knew everyone, but when meeting others, establishing your tribe and your private name was necessary. Pointing to himself, he named his tribe, but it seemed lost to the white mans' ears. They weren't familiar with the over seven hundred aboriginal languages currently on this great island. When his announcement elicited no response, he tried again, this time speaking slowly.

"What do you think he's sayin'?" one of the men asked, watching the Aborigine carefully. Most of their previous experiences with Aborigines were distant sightings on a hillside as they ran from them. The few they interacted with on the various stations had been reasonably domesticated, but this one was obviously wild, and they all wondered what he wanted.

"Let's offer him some food and see if that satisfies 'im," someone stated, and the cook got up from where he was sitting. This sudden movement nearly startled Omeo into running, but he firmly stood his ground, watching the many men warily.

"I say just kill 'em all," another man contributed belligerently. His tone was heard by all, and Omeo understood the underlying threat, even if he didn't understand the words. He glanced at the man warily, wondering at his anger.

"He ain't done nothin' yet," someone else contributed but held his musket primed and ready, just in case. He glanced around. "Think 'e's alone?"

"They don't travel in large groups, just families," someone contributed knowledgeably. They were all a little unnerved.

The cook approached Omeo with a plate of food and a spoon, gesturing towards it as he held it out.

Omeo stared at him curiously, wondering at the man. What he offered did not look like food to Omeo. He could smell the fatty mutton, which was too rich for him to eat, but he watched the man warily in case it was a trap. He saw the spoon and the plate, and his heart leapt into his throat. This was the white man's stone he sought! He gingerly took the offering with his free hand, still watching for any sign of a trap. Once the plate was in his hand, he stared at the contents uncomprehendingly. The food did not look appealing to him in the least, but the metal of the spoon and plate did. He leaned his spear against his shoulder to free up his other hand, keeping it close enough that he could put it into action quickly if he needed it, and he began to examine the coveted metal.

"He ain't eatin'," someone commented.

"I don't think he came to us for food," another put in, watching avidly at the strange man and his actions.

The spoon was the easiest to handle, and he picked it up and turned it over. He knew he could file it to a point, which he would need for a spear, but it was much smaller than he wanted. *Maybe the other thing would work,* he thought, turning the plate over and allowing the food to drop off as he examined the other side.

"Hey!" the cook, who had backed up to give the wild man some room, protested loudly at his good food being wasted on the ground.

"He ain't here for food," one of the original speakers put in before the cook's anger could escalate. "I think he wants the metal plate. You know, he don' look like the Aborigines nearer Sydney; he ain't tame like 'em."

"We got some beads and stuff in the trade goods," the cook put in, annoyed that his food wasn't being appreciated.

"I think he would prefer a hand axe or metal for making spears," another observed, all of them holding tightly to their firearms in case this was merely a distraction. Several looked uneasily into the night, away from the spectacle of the Aborigine examining the plate and spoon.

"How do you know?"

"He's lookin' at that plate and spoon pretty hard."

"I don't care what 'e wants, let's chase him off," the belligerent man gestured with his musket uneasily.

"What do you think 'e's got in trade?"

"Ain't got nothin' on 'im." That was obvious since he was essentially naked and had only his spear in his possession.

They watched as the wild man examined the tin plate and spoon minutely, touching it reverently with his fingertips. It was obvious he coveted the fine metal. He finally looked up and gestured, the gesture lost on the more verbal men. Omar quietly grunted a word in his language, but that was ignored as well since they either didn't understand it or didn't hear it. Frustrated, he moved to leave, taking the plate and spoon with him.

"Hey!" the cook called, causing Omeo to stop in surprise. The man took a couple of strides and wrenched the plate and spoon from his hand forcefully. He stared at the white man for a moment, intending to take them back, but he was shoved away.

"He don' understan'," one of the men argued but already several men had risen and were gesturing with their muskets. Together, they chased Omeo off. He had looked like he might fight the cook for the metals in his hands. His fierce and wild looks, unnatural to the men, frightened them on a basic level.

"Get gone!"

"Shoo!"

"Hiya!"

"Get along with you."

"Maybe we should shoot him and be done with it."

Omeo ended up running off into the night when the large white men frightened him. Maybe the metal they had shown him wasn't a gift. Anything that valuable surely wouldn't be given away, and now, he was confused. What could he do to obtain some of the white man's metal? They hadn't spoken in a way that he could understand. He had found their noises loud and unnecessary in the still night air. They made too much noise, like a baby, and he didn't comprehend any of their words. He carefully made his way back to his family, thinking over his interactions with the white men and how to overcome them.

The carters were uneasy, doubling the guard after their encounter with the wild Aborigine. Who knew how many were out there in the night? Australian nights and the Outback were already mysterious enough, and they all were looking forward to getting back to the city with its lights and people. They built up the fire unreasonably high, wasting the sparse wood they had found.

The next day, the men saw that they hadn't scared off the Aborigine completely. He was following them, occasionally paralleling their course on the winding road that ribboned across the Outback, connecting various stations and towns with civilization.

"He's got a family with 'im," one of the men mentioned, spotting them moving along the nearby hills.

"You got good eyesight, Sam," one of the other men grunted. "If 'e's got 'is wife and family with 'im, maybe we should hunt 'em," he smiled, showing uneven, brown teeth. Then he spit the tobacco from his mouth onto the side of the road.

"I'll go along with that. Might provide us with some fun," another man put in after hearing the conversation.

"We got to get these carts back to Sydney. We don't have time to be wasting," another man pointed out, trying to keep his men in line.

"Oh, one day ain't gonna hurt none. We need some excitement."

"We could share the woman. There weren't none on that last station."

George Granger looked at the men disgustedly. He knew what kind of fun they meant. They would hunt the Aborigine down and kill him, if they could. Then, if he had a wife with him, they would rape her for the fun of it. He couldn't see the family clearly, but Sam had. Usually, you could easily spot aboriginal children with their distinctive, blonde hair that eventually turned to black. "Just do your job," he advised, wondering how he could get them to stop thinking about the man and his family. He didn't hold with some people's beliefs that Aborigine people weren't human and didn't own the land, but he knew better than

to voice his opinions. He had a job to do. They'd collected the bags of wool, and it was his job to get them to Sydney where they would be loaded on ships and delivered to English mills that would turn the wool into cloth. He would only be paid when he delivered everything to the factor in Sydney. He couldn't pay his men if he didn't do that, and he didn't want them to waste precious time hunting Aborigines. He knew many of the men who hired on for these long trips didn't realize how long they would be gone. They didn't understand the many months it would take to reach some of these more remote stations, and they didn't realize they would be without lights and the comforts of the big city for so long. Some were depraved individuals, who disappeared into the Outback, using fake names and committing crimes in the city they were escaping from. Many were former convicts or the offspring of convicts, but he couldn't be too choosy as he needed men to drive the many carts and wagons, handle the oxen and bullocks pulling them, and help get the bales of wool to market. Not all of them were of this ilk, but George couldn't afford to be too choosy as he needed to get the work done and many were unwilling to go into the vast Outback, which frightened them.

Over the next couple days, several of the men talked of nothing else but hunting the Aborigine and his family that they still occasionally saw on the hills. It was determined there were four in the family: two adults and two children. The children were shorter, although one of them was nearly the size of the adults. They couldn't make out the sex of the children, but someone had confirmed one adult was a woman, and this led to speculation about whether they could separate the male from his female for their own enjoyment. They talked as though the Aborigines were not people, although they clearly were human in

appearance and what they planned to do to the woman also spoke against this.

"You don't own me, Granger!" one man, Eli Sprecher, told him in a sneering voice.

"I'm paying you to cart these bundles to market for me, not chase after women!"

"We ain't had a day off in months, George," another tried to reason.

"You'll get your days off when we get this," he pointed to the ungainly bundles piled high on the wagons, "to Sydney."

"Another day or two ain't gonna matter."

The arguments went around and round at the fire nightly, and when they stopped for their noon, the men continued to speculate and use the Aborigines as a topic of conversation. George really began to see some of the true personalities come out of men he had thought were hard workers. Not all wanted to participate and chase after the Aborigine family, and he respected them a hell of a lot more than the ones who did. Fortunately, the ones who participated were a minority.

That minority disappeared before breakfast the following day, so they could not continue their journey. Several of the missing men were needed to drive the large wagons and carts and handle the bullocks pulling them.

"God dammit!" George swore when he realized he was short-handed. If the men didn't return soon, they were going to have to tie the guard horses to the wagons and use the guards to drive the wagons and carts. He was tempted to just do that anyway but couldn't abandon the men to the Outback. He knew without food, which they weren't even thinking about right now, they would starve to death, and that was a horrible death for anyone. Knowing these types of men, he realized

they wouldn't make it back, and he knew his reputation as a carter would be destroyed.

CHAPTER THREE

The family couldn't understand Omeo's decision to parallel the odd caravan, and they would never question it. Each had seen the strange animals and understood they weren't some weird aberration but merely animals they weren't familiar with. Horses were not common to their area of the Outback and neither were the white men controlling them. The smells that floated on the air were foreign to the Aborigines and unpleasant, but they wouldn't disobey him, and when he had returned that night, he seemed excited, agitated, and thoughtful. He didn't discuss his thoughts with them. It wasn't their place.

Omeo was trying to figure out what he had done wrong and how he could obtain the coveted metals. He had seen one of those white man's stone axes leaning against some of the wood they were cutting for their fire. It had just been left there in the open for anyone to touch, and he wondered at something so valuable being left unguarded like that. Apparently, the white men didn't value it as much as he, and he hoped he could find something to exchange for it.

He had watched the white men avidly in the days following his unsuccessful visit. He allowed them to see him and his family on the hillside but stayed well away from them, so they were no threat. That morning, he had gotten up early in order to hunt for a kangaroo. He was hoping to find a way to convey that he would trade the meat for some of the coveted metals. He hoped they would see that he meant no harm and that the kangaroo he was now bringing them would express that he wished to trade and bargain. He didn't see the white men who had left early in the morning darkness from their overly large fire, but they saw him and hid. When Omeo finally became aware of the smell of the white men over the smell of the blood of the kangaroo, it was too late. He found himself hit with the butt of a musket and went down without a fight.

"You killed him, Sam!"

"I don't care. Let's find his woman and have some fun."

"What if she's ugly?"

"Who cares? A cat's a cat in the dark, right?" another quipped crudely.

"I say who finds 'er first, gets to say who gets 'er," another challenged, speeding up to be the one to find the coveted woman, who was now essentially unprotected.

"We are gonna share," Sam threatened, hurrying after the others.

"I say, whoever catches her, gets to say," another taunted, and they all hurried along, unaware they were making a lot of noise in the still morning air. It wasn't loud to the white men, who still snored around

their fire, but the animals and the Aborigines, who were in tune with nature, heard them.

Miro, Alinta's brother, was dozing in the early morning. Charged with guarding their family, he was used to the sounds of the night, but in his slumber, he barely heard the white men, who had caught the slight smell of their campfire. He was knocked out before he was able to come completely awake, the butt of the musket catching him unawares along the side of his head. Only his thick hair and the darkness prevented them from bashing in his skull. Still, it would be a long time before he awoke from his unnatural slumber.

Alinta woke, hearing the white men, and she tried to scream as she saw the men looming over the small fire burning in the hollow where they chose to camp. She kicked at her mother to wake her as she quickly got up to run. The men gleefully ran after her and several stopped the older one from leaving, assuming it must be her dam. Their eyes left her with no questions as to their intentions. Sam and the others of his ilk took turns, taking their time raping the older woman as the other two, Eli and Bradley, went after the younger one.

Alinta dodged in and out of the spinifex, the tall grasses, and the trees. The men, delighted, whooped and followed, frightening her and causing her to become careless as she ran for all she was worth. It was a long time before they tired her young body with their cat and mouse games.

"I got her!" Bradley crowed, having leapt and tackled her. Alinta fought like a wild thing! It was unnatural for her to disobey a man, but these men were nothing like she was used to, and they frightened her. After several minutes of struggle, Eli produced some piggin' strings,

and they tied both her hands and her feet. The rope around her neck was unnecessary but she fought them all the way.

"You don't wanna take 'er now?" Eli asked the younger man, envious of his capture but not in the least interested in raping the young woman. She didn't appeal to him at all with her skinny body; he preferred meat on a woman's bones…more cushion. This almost straight up form reminded him too much of a boy, and his normally randy cock shriveled at the thought of touching the young, aboriginal woman.

"No, I'm gonna savor 'er," he said with a cheeky grin. Excited by the capture and her struggling against him, he had a raging hard-on from his exertions. He would have taken her then and there but didn't want an audience. There was a tent stored in with the supplies, and he intended to use it when he got her back to camp. "Let's see if the others have had their fill of the dam." Throwing her easily over his shoulder, the men slowly made their way back towards the Aborigine camp, surprised to see the boy still laying on the ground where he had been guarding the others.

Inala, Alinta's dam, lay in a tight ball after having been violated many times by the men who had captured her. She hurt inside in ways she had never felt before. Never had her mate taken her over and over so brutally as these white men had.

"We better go," Bradley put in as they came up, slipping the woman off his shoulder. Eli helped to hold her between them as Bradley released her feet.

"You gonna share 'er?" Sam asked, eyeing the young woman and instantly getting hard again. It had been exciting to take the reluctant, older woman time and again in the space of a few short minutes. She

had fought at first but eventually resigned herself to her fate, and that had made it less exciting. The fight was what he wanted, and he could see the young woman was still fighting her bonds as the two men held her effortlessly.

"Nope, finders keepers, and I caught her," Bradley answered, ready to take on the older man, who he didn't like. This search for the Aborigines had been the older man's idea, and Bradley had gone along for the excitement, giving up valuable hours of sleep that he needed.

"I think you should share," Sam said as he got up cautiously and eyed the younger man and the woman. He stared at her in a lust-filled haze, the bulge in his pants obvious.

"Nope, she's mine." Bradley's tone brooked no interference, and he eyed the man warily. He was ready for Sam when he lunged, a knife suddenly appearing in his hand. Bradley pushed the girl into Eli's surprised arms as he slapped the knife aside and lunged at the older man to unbalance him, attempting to wrestle the knife away and tripping him in the process. He needn't have worried. The man fell on his own knife and turned over with a groan, the knife protruding from his gut. "Oh, shit, Sam. Now, look at what you've done!"

Sam looked down at the knife in his stomach and went to pull it.

"Don't!" Bradley tried staying the hand, but he was too late. Sam yanked the knife out and blood spurted. Holding his hand down on the wound, Bradley could only watch as the man quickly bled to death from his self-inflicted wound.

The others stared down in horror. The altercation had taken place so quickly.

"We better bury him," Eli said, holding the struggling girl, who was looking about at the white men, eyes wide with fear as she attempted to get free. He calmly slapped her with the back of his hand to quiet her struggles.

"We better get back to Granger before he goes on without us," another pointed out. The sun was coming up, and he knew they were derelict in their duties to the man.

"Shouldn't we bury Sam?" another repeated Eli's comment.

"We ain't got time. Go through his pockets and see if he has anything worthwhile. I claim his gear," Eli stated.

"I fought him," Bradley said, suddenly rising from where he was kneeling by the corpse, realizing he better make his wishes known before the other men took everything, including the woman. "I get his gear. You can have what's on 'im," he indicated the corpse and went to take the young woman away from Eli. "I'll go on ahead and let Granger know we are on our way."

"What about 'er?" one of the men indicated the older woman.

"Bring 'er along. We can use her on the way."

A couple rifled through Sam's pockets for anything of value, finding only a few coins and a pocketknife but nothing else. By turning the corpse over, they hid the knife that had killed him from their own view. They left it and the body to the elements as they rose to take the older woman, forcing her to walk with them after tying her hands as she began to feebly struggle. They passed the still unconscious boy and ignored him, leaving him to whatever the fates had in store for him. They eventually passed by the older man as well. Omeo was lying there, trying but unable to rise as the ache in his head sorted itself. Inala and Alinta, prisoners of the white men, stared in horror at his supine form but were pulled roughly along.

"What have you got there?" George asked gruffly, seeing the men coming into camp with the two women. Taking a second look, he realized one looked like a girl.

"Prisoners. Spoils of war," one of the men quipped, grinning.

"Where's Sam?"

"He got killed," they told him but didn't tell him the fight was with Bradley. "His body's out there."

George, anxious to get underway, already had the oxen and bullocks harnessed and the horses saddled. "Grab some grub, and let's get going," he ordered, disgusted with whatever had happened to allow these men to take possession of these women. He knew there was nothing he could do short of ordering them to release the two Aborigine women, but he didn't want a mutiny on his hands, so he decided to ignore the situation. It was later, when some of the men fought over the right to have the older woman, that he regretted not insisting they leave the women where they had found them. They headed out, the dust kicked up by their wagons, carts, bullocks, oxen, and horses settling over the desert as they left this spot behind. All day long, they plodded along. On a good day they would make twenty miles, only ten miles on a bad day. Today, was a good day despite the delay in setting off.

Word spread between the men that Bradley had killed Sam over the young girl, and no one challenged his right to keep her for himself, but they kept that from George for the time being. Bradley asked for the tent from supplies and got it set up. Before he took the girl into the tent to exert what he felt were his rights, he tried to feed her mutton and biscuit, which she refused. She fought him, knowing what he wanted but not understanding how it worked. She had seen her mother taken repeatedly by her father over the years, so the rapes of the men today were nothing. Now, she resigned herself to enduring what she expected was to become the norm.

"You are mine now," the man said, but Alinta didn't understand his utterings. She had never heard this language before, and to her it was gibberish. The look in his eye though, that was universal. She had seen such looks at the gatherings. Her father and mother had both worked hard to keep the men away from her at these events, but she didn't believe anyone could save her this time. She thought she could see what he wanted in his look, and when he grabbed her arm, she knew she wasn't wrong.

The thought of him touching her was repugnant. He smelled so unlike the men she had grown up with and expected to one day belong to. His sweat was sharp and foreign, and the white of his skin was different from anything she had ever known. She looked around and the leers on the faces of the other men told their tale. They knew what Bradley had in mind for her. There was no hope for it. Alinta resigned herself to whatever the fates had decided for her.

With her lack of clothing, it wasn't hard for him to simply unbutton his trousers and take her when his lust was high. He didn't think of her enjoyment or her satisfaction, she was simply satisfying *his* lust. He didn't think of the fact that she might be a virgin and unused to a man's touch. He didn't consider that she wasn't aroused and there would be little, if any, lubrication, so it would be painful. He pumped into her time and time again, spitting on his cock and forcing his way inside as he assuaged his own needs and his own desires, not stopping until he was satisfied. He held onto her as she cried silently, panting at his exertions, and when she was done crying, he took her again and again.

She was quite sore the next day. The blood had dried on her legs and it hurt to pee, but over the next couple weeks, she learned to quietly accept what he took without regard to her feelings…she learned it was useless to fight.

Inala was concerned about her son and mate. She had seen them lying on the ground as these white men took the women back to their camp. As they took her over and again, she was resigned, but she worried about her daughter as she watched the young man, a strong one from what she could see, take her into the shelter he had erected. She knew what his intentions were as he held the woman proprietarily. She saw the blood on her daughter's leg the next day and tried to explain about keeping herself clean, but Alinta did not want to listen. She didn't want to eat, and she didn't want to clean herself. Maybe if she died, she would be free. She became despondent.

Inala watched as Alinta began to fade away in the coming weeks, and the man who owned her finally noticed as well. He held Alinta and forced a noxious liquid down her throat, only to have it come back up violently from her gut. After that, he offered her mutton and bread, which she would have normally refused, but he indicated the black bottle of liquid he would force down her throat again, and she reluctantly began to eat. After that, she knew she wouldn't die as quickly as she wanted.

At the next town, Bradley took Alinta to a startled blacksmith, who fastened a collar around her neck. He hammered the pin in and made chains for the pleased carter, who held them proprietarily while he also made cuffs for the girl's ankles, chaining her legs so she couldn't run far. One of the men who felt he owned the older woman envied the look, and he had a similar set made for his captive.

CHAPTER FOUR

Omeo was the first to awaken. He struggled to rise but wisely stayed down when the white men returned. He recognized the footfalls of his mate and daughter among the others but couldn't open his eyes wide enough to look. The pain in his head was incredible. Gradually, he got up, his head throbbing painfully as he made his way to the rise and watched the white men put the women in among the wagons and head out. It was only then he thought of his son and began to make his way painfully to where Miro lay. He was just coming to after many hours of unconsciousness. Luckily, he woke just in time as the dingoes, drawn to the scent of the dead white man, were out hunting in the early morning hours.

Omeo was pleased by the knife he found in the white man and the fine leather belt he tugged from around the man's waist. The shirt was

ruined with blood, but his pants, boots, and even his stinking socks were useful, so they gathered these and bound them together with the belt. Father and son headed out slowly, following the tracks of the wagons on the winding road and carrying the unfamiliar gathering bags and water urn that were normally carried by the women. They weren't used to carrying burdens, normally keeping their hands free to hunt and carry their spears. When Miro felt better, Omeo tasked him with most of these items, feeling he was too important to be carrying women's items as he searched for his wife and daughter. Because they were incapacitated and had to travel on foot, it took them longer to catch up to the wagons.

"We're being followed," one of the men reported to George Granger a week later.

"Followed?" he repeated worriedly. Just what he needed, bushrangers—men who had escaped from prison or gone wild—were notorious for stealing from the unwary, but their company was too big and well-armed for bushrangers to bother with the carters.

"Yeah, I think it's them women's menfolk."

George sighed. He thought the men were content now that they had their women on the long trip from the Outback. They were on their way back to Sydney with their full wagons and still had at least a month of travel. Even men he had thought morally incapable had availed themselves of the older woman. Bradley wasn't sharing his captive, which caused some resentment among the men. The men who captured the older woman were whoring her out, collecting cash money

or trinkets in exchange for her favors. One or two of the men wanting to buy her services were borrowing against their future pay in order to have their time with the woman. It was a horrible experience for her, but there was nothing George could do about it, short of putting the men who owned her out of their caravan, and until they were closer to civilization, he didn't dare consider it. He knew some of the men were dangerous and could become violent if he even risked suggesting it. Until they were closer to civilization, where there were legal repercussions and their violence could be met with justice, he didn't dare confront them about the women. Besides, he needed them to work, and they could not be replaced out here.

"Chase them off but don't kill them," he ordered his outer guards. He later heard gunfire and hoped they were shooting at the Aborigines, just merely trying to scare them. They were limited on their ammunition too, so he didn't want the guards to waste too much.

Both Alinta and Inala heard the gunfire, and it was frightening as they didn't understand it. They were barely surviving amidst these men. Inala accepted her body being used, but she worried about her daughter. Keeping her daughter alive was paramount to the older woman. After they had traveled on for weeks, Inala noticed changes in her daughter, changes only someone in tune with their body and nature could fathom. It would be months before it would become obvious, but her daughter's flow had stopped after just one month of being held captive and being used by the man in the tent.

Having nothing to do all day but sit and wait for the nights when the men would take her, Inala had nothing but time to think and plan. They had tied her so she couldn't get away, using some of the precious white man's stone to hold her in a painful vise around her ankles and fashioning a collar as well. Her daughter had a similar set, which chafed her beautiful skin. The man who held her daughter used the animal's wool to pad the stone and prevent painful sores underneath it, but they didn't think of doing that for Inala, and her ring was now deeply rooted in her neck and cutting into the skin.

Almost daily, the guards tried to chase off the determined Aborigines who followed them, shooting closer and closer to the man and boy. A ricochet off some stone finally made them disappear into the brush. Omeo and Miro made sure to remain invisible to the men from then on but crept closer and closer at night. Omeo finally managed to free Inala one night after the last man who had taken her cruelly fell asleep next to her, snoring with his mouth open. Omeo pulled her along, taking with him several of the white men's stones as well as the axe, which was again left haphazardly by the chopped wood as he had observed on his first visit. When Inala would have protested and gone back for Alinta, Omeo refused. To him, his daughter was ruined and was of no further value to him. He had what he had come for. The men's use of his mate was nothing. It was only as her belly began to swell months later that he reconsidered his decision to rescue her. Still, the white man's stone was valuable, and he didn't regret the loss of his only daughter, considering her a fair exchange for the white man's stone he had taken with him. At one time, Alinta had been valuable to him, but now, she was useless, and he left her behind without another thought. After all, he could have other daughters; he still had his mate.

"Get up! Get up! The woman is gone!" one of the guards called, kicking at a couple of the men to rouse them.

The consternation of the guards was heightened by their embarrassment. They were bewildered that someone—they were sure it was the man who had been following them and had been in their camp—had stolen the woman, their only distraction on this long trip, and had also made off with an axe, a pot, and several odd pieces of metal. Security was tightened and only the fact that Bradley felt he owned Alinta kept her from being ravaged. She had been in their tent together and protected by the brawny man.

"Can anyone sew?" Bradley asked a few days later as they made their way east and a little south, heading for Sydney. Signs of civilization were obvious along the trail as their wagons and carts lumbered along. Occasionally, station owners, their wives, and even their whole families including children came to meet the carters, curious about the news or gossip they might impart. Bradley had been the subject of several obvious stares of disapproval for his ownership of the captured woman. Her state of undress hadn't bothered him before they passed through Menindee, but they were seeing more signs of settlement the farther east they went, and he was becoming more uncomfortable with it.

Between the men, they came up with a shirt to cover the young woman's naked frame. It was a bit long, falling below her knees. For the first time since her capture, Alinta took an interest in her surroundings. Her mother's disappearance had further distressed her, but she knew why her father hadn't freed her. Her value had been in her virtue, and he had abandoned her now that it was gone. Bereft of her family, she would have faded away, but now, she looked about her and began trying to figure out how she could escape her captor, wondering if she dared try. The shirt pleased her. She'd never felt material like this before, and she knew the shirt hid her nakedness from the men who looked at her with lust in their eyes. Only the fact that Bradley was young, had made his claim, and would apparently back it up with a fight to the death, kept the other men at bay. She had seen how they had used her dam, and the thought of entertaining that many of the men made her shudder.

"What are you going to do with 'er when we get to Sydney?" George asked Bradley one night by the fire.

"I'll sell her to a brothel I know. They will like her dusky skin," he grinned, showing no repentance for his behavior, feeling it was his due. After all, she was *only* an Aborigine. He was a man, he had needs, and she fulfilled them. He was glad she didn't bleed, so he could take her when he felt like it. He did not realize the significance of this fact. Young and virile, he delighted in the envy of his fellow carters over his obvious enjoyment of the young and nubile woman.

Alinta desperately wanted to clean herself of the smells of the white man who used her continually. She didn't understand his need but accepted it as his male right. She didn't welcome the invasion of her body and remembered her mother's advice about enticing this act from her man, but she felt no need to entice *him*. She was young, and she had healed from his initial invasions. It no longer hurt, and for that she was grateful. She no longer bled after his repeated invasions of her body, but she also wasn't aware of the significance of her monthly leaving and didn't recognize the obvious beginning signs of a pregnancy. She was too young for a pregnancy, but her body knew

what was needed, and as she was eating regularly now, it took the available nourishment needed to nourish the fetus.

George hid his disgust over the young man's cavalier treatment of the young woman. He had to shrug it off, feeling it wasn't any of his business, but he knew he would never hire this young man again. Despite his good looks, his winning attitude around the men not trying to buy time with the woman he had captured, and his brute strength, he was still an ass. He had also cost them the life of one man, unceremoniously claiming that man's possessions. Hidden in those possessions, Bradley had found a roll of bills, which he secreted away, telling no one about them. Whatever Sam had been into, he had hidden from his fellow carters, and Bradley felt the money was well-earned. The girl was a treat, and he knew he'd also get some good money from the brothel for her. All in all, this trip would be very profitable for the young man.

CHAPTER FIVE

The closer they got to Sydney, the more traffic they encountered. Other carters were going out to collect from wool drayage companies, who in turn took merchandise out to Menindee and other outlying towns and villages as settlements became more common along this track. Stations became more frequent and smaller, and herds of animals crowded the roads on their way to market. It was nice to see people again. Most were friendly, or if they weren't friendly, at least they ignored each other.

One day as they approached Bathurst, thrilled with how close they were to Sydney, they came across an enormous herd of sheep being taken to the Outback. They had encountered smaller flocks but nothing like this. It was a massive flock, probably ten thousand sheep, and all of them were prime Merino sheep. The sheep were shorn close and had obviously been purchased after their value dropped with the shearing. The men were surprised to learn the owner was an American woman with a dark complexion. She was stunningly beautiful, but they were kept well at bay by her men, called vaqueros, who showed off their expertise with their whips. One of them had a forty-foot-long whip that he expertly cracked above the heads of the sheep, keeping them moving along at a good clip as other men and dogs kept the large herd surging forward. The cavalcade of wagons carrying their wool had pulled into a circle for the night near a large field. They set up camp, their bullocks and horses contained in the center.

"Hello, the camp," one of the riders, a large dark-haired man, hailed them. "Mind if we camp nearby?" he called with a distinctive American twang.

"Plenty of grass," George pointed out, the meadow beside their own camp more than large enough to accommodate the huge flock of sheep. It was then he saw the herd of black horses that had been trotting behind the enormous flock. They were magnificent, and he couldn't remember seeing such fine stock before. All his men stood up from their various positions to watch as the woman, who was obviously in charge, brought the herd in. Her men quickly erected a fold for the sheep using rope and any available brush to enclose them, then spaced men and dogs around the sheep and horses as they bedded them down for the night. The far side of the meadow contained a stream, and they slowly herded smaller groups of sheep to it, so they could drink their fill before being rotated back into the enormous flock. The many wagons and carts of a cartage company that was traveling with them went to one side of the meadow and set up another camp.

"I'm George Granger, and these are my men," he said by way of introduction to the woman and her men. He stared at her beauty. He was certain she wasn't an American because her accent was so interesting.

"I am Senora Mary Carmen Valenzuela Pearson," she stated, giving it the full flavor and inflection of her Spanish heritage while looking at him as though he were an equal, and this surprised him. "These are my men, and this is our friend, Mel Lawrence, who is accompanying us." She pointed out the men who wore odd, short, little jackets, wide hats, and tight pants. The last one she introduced was a large man riding a different horse from theirs, a former Brumby from what he could tell. The man, who was pulling several packhorses that were also Brumbies, nodded coldly, glancing around the camp as he went to put up his horses. He had been the one asking if they could camp nearby.

"You got a station in the Outback?" George inquired jovially of the owner, hoping to be thought of as charming and curry her favor, if not as a possible suitor, then perhaps as a business connection. With this many sheep, the possibility of hauling supplies and wool was always there.

"I am heading for Twin Station," she told him, waiting to see if he would react to her admission or if the name of the station elicited a response. He didn't react.

"I haven't heard of it," he admitted, shaking his head. "There's plenty of 'em out there," he gestured towards the land about them, encompassing it all, "and you must have a lot of land to handle a flock like that one." He pointed his thumb over his shoulder at the sheep that were even now cropping at the grass before laying down and settling in for the night, their legs tucked under their bodies.

"Oh, they aren't all mine. Half the sheep belong to our neighbor there, Mel Lawrence," she nodded towards the man who was even now unsaddling his mount and glanced over at hearing his name mentioned.

"You have a station out there?" George called to him, raising his voice to span the distance between them.

Mel shook his head. "No, I'm going out to claim my own space," he informed him, turning to put his saddle down next to one of the wagons before reaching for the pack saddles on the other horses.

"There's a lot of land out there for the taking," George admitted, nodding musingly and wondering at Mel's American accent. He wondered if the man had a lot of money in order to buy all these sheep but reminded himself again how cheap sheep were right after shearing.

"I've convinced Mr. Lawrence to travel with us and take a look at land adjoining our own station," the woman informed him.

"Sooner know your neighbors, eh?" he asked, wondering if he could convince her to hire him to take them supplies and return with their wool. The company he worked for would appreciate additional convoys of supplies, added men, and the wool.

"Mind if we share your fire? We have our own supplies and foodstuffs," she said, indicating the wagons and carts that even now were pulling into the far side of the clearing.

"Please do," he said, delighted.

She got down and a man was there instantly to lead her horse away. He was a fine beast, and George was impressed to realize it was a stallion. Women, in his experience, didn't ride stallions. Its body was strong, sturdy, and tall, and it looked like he had staying power. The brute quickly established that this was *his* herd as he acted up for the man holding his bridle, making it difficult for him to control.

As Carmen sat down by the fire, a few of the men got up and tipped their hats as they introduced themselves. Any that didn't get up in her presence were nudged by their compatriots as they too got up and acknowledged the lady. Mel Lawrence watched knowingly, taking in the manners of the various men and shaking hands with several of them as they introduced themselves. One man especially drew Mel's gaze. He was behaving in a proprietorial way, holding a chain, which led to a collar around the neck of an aboriginal woman. Mel noted the additional chains around her ankles as well. She hadn't seen too much of slavery, although she had traveled in the south of America to New Orleans.

The newcomers took a while to get settled due to the large number of animals and people traveling together, and when they finally settled, dogs and men were scattered to guard their animals. George learned that Senora Pearson was a widow from central California, who had inherited a station in the Outback with her cousins and was making her way there with some new stock intending to resettle her family. He was surprised to meet her three fine sons and daughter. She didn't look old enough to have so many children.

Mel talked with a few of the Australian carters, who told stories of the long journey from the Outback. He learned they had caught some Aborigines, and this was where the chained woman came from. Bradley saw Mel's interest and made it clear *his woman* wasn't for rent or sale. "Would any of you like to play cards?" Mel suggested blandly, pushing aside any resentment at the man's immediate assumption that he wanted his woman. Mel pulled a deck of cards from his saddlebags and began to shuffle them, drawing the men's eyes to them.

Bradley and several of the men eagerly agreed to play, and a few of the vaqueros joined in. Mel sucked on one of the pipes he had bought in Sydney, the delicious aroma from the tobacco leaf eddying in the air as he contemplated his cards. A couple of the men, long without their tobacco, or dundeen as they called it, bought some figs of tobacco from the American. As the cooks brought around their food, players dropped out to eat dinner. Mel ate while coolly playing several hands. He could assess the men and their cards and easily counted them while figuring the odds of what they possibly held in their hands and betting accordingly. Mel could see that Bradley thought himself a decent card player, his good looks and demeanor showing him to be a braggart and a showman. His treatment of the Aborigine showed Mel that his character was not what he presented to others.

Mel assessed the man, and his heart went out to the woman, knowing she submitted only because of the chain around her neck and ankles. Mel bided his time playing cards until one by one, the vaqueros dropped out and then the Australians. Murmurs in the background indicated that George was still talking with the Senora by the fire. Mel grinned, knowing Carmen only used her full name like that to confuse men. In America she had been simply Carmen Pearson and didn't use her mother's full family name of Senora Mary Carmen Valenzuela Pearson. Mel understood and knew the men with Carmen understood, but men such as George Granger and others of his kind were impressed by English titles and would not understand.

"Ah, that's the last of my coin!" Bradley exclaimed, throwing down his cards as he lost once again. He'd played long enough that he'd lost all his own money plus the roll he had found in Sam's gear. Several of

the men who worked with him noticed he stayed in the game a long time, and they wondered why he had so much cash money on him.

Mel restrained a smile as he raked in the winnings. He had learned how to play cards in New Orleans from masters. He'd let the Australian think he was winning many times, but he was simply a bad card player and was being strung along by a superior card player. "Tell you what, I'm inclined to keep playing. Would you consider playing some more?"

"I hain't got nuthin' to play with," the carter admitted ruefully, rubbing his chin and feeling the stubble that had built up since the previous river crossing when he had last taken the time to shave.

"Don't you?" Mel inquired, his glance following the chain towards the woman sitting nearby. Mel had watched as Bradley gave her a plate of food. There had been a brief pause when he had reached for a bottle in his shirt pocket, then the woman hastily ate. Mel wondered what was in the bottle.

"I told you I ain't rentin' 'er out," Bradley said, sounding morose.

"I'm not talking about rentin'," Mel admitted. "How much would you say she's worth?" Mel heard a slight gasp behind them when the children's nanny heard the offer. Mel glanced back, but the woman was looking decidedly away. Mel could tell she didn't approve. Mel also glanced at the children, who were playing with one of the young dogs that wasn't occupied guarding sheep. Mel pretended no interest in whether Bradley wanted to continue playing or not.

Bradley considered for a moment. He had been drinking a lot that evening, seemingly a necessity when playing cards. He named a price that sounded outrageous, and Mel grinned knowingly.

"You wouldn't get that in no brothel in the city," Mel answered, having heard of the man's plans. He shuffled the cards, being careful not to give away his expertise, although he did know some fancy shuffles. Mel also knew how to deal from the bottom of the deck and a few other tricks that he hadn't had to enact to beat this man at poker. Mel made a move to put away the cards, then looked around. "Anyone else want to play?" he called. Several shook their heads. They had lost just enough, although a few of the vaqueros had won because they knew not to keep playing with the American for too long.

"How much would you give me in credit for 'er?" Bradley asked as Mel went to put away the cards.

Mel named a sum that was less than half what Bradley had stated, and when he didn't respond immediately, he made to get up, putting the large stack of bills he had won from the man in his shirt pocket.

"Alright, I'll play. I'll win too," Bradley bragged as Mel sat back down and handed the deck to him to shuffle and deal. Bradley tried to cheat, but he was so bad at it that Mel easily beat him at his game. Slowly and methodically over the next few hours, he lost every other hand. The winning hands were enough to keep him hopeful that his next hand would be a big win. He was losing a little more with each play until finally, he was out of money once again. "Well, that's it," he finally said, having lost to an inside straight. He shook his head. He thought the American had cheated but couldn't figure out how, and his own attempts at cheating had been in vain. Still, he had won enough that he thought he could beat the American. He rose to leave the area.

"Now, wait a minute. Aren't you forgetting something?" Mel asked, rising too and feeling the numbness in his legs from sitting too

long. He hoped it passed quickly. This could get ugly fast, and he had to be ready.

"Forgetting what?" Bradley tried to hedge, but several of the carters were looking at him with disgust. Maybe it wasn't for them to judge that he had fought with Sam and killed him, but to renege on a bet that they had all witnessed wasn't good.

"You borrowed against your woman there," Mel pointed out.

"I...didn't..." he began belligerently, then seeing the looks on the men's faces in the firelight as he looked away from Mel's pointed gaze, he shrugged and reluctantly handed the chain over. He walked away, disgusted with himself as the woman looked at the chain and the new man holding it. This was unprecedented. Never had the white man given her to someone else. She had no comprehension of the cards they had been playing and was merely waiting until the man would demand her presence in the hated tent.

Alinta hadn't noticed the other white man, not daring to look at any other man since Bradley's possessiveness caused fights. She hadn't understood any of their verbal exchanges, but she understood that the new man holding her chain was her new owner, and she glanced at the man, sensing something no one else around the fire did. As her eyes traveled up the chain to the hands of the man now holding it loosely in his hands, she wondered if Bradley had given her away for the night or if he had grown tired of her.

Mel rose and beckoned to the woman, being careful not to pull on the chain. The woman looked surprised. Normally, Bradley had grabbed her arm, pushed her in the direction he wanted her to go, or pulled on her chain. She got up hesitantly, and Mel beckoned again, slipping his pack of cards into his pocket as he gathered the coins and

bills of various countries in the pile and put his winnings deep in another pocket.

Alinta followed Mel as he headed for his ground-hitched horses and gear. Mel rummaged in the supplies and pulled out a blanket roll and a ground sheet, spreading them out next to the saddle. He rummaged some more as Alinta looked on, wondering at the many unfamiliar things. Mel made another bed next to the first. He pointed at the first bed and then to Alinta. Next, he pointed at the second bed and to himself. Alinta's eyes opened wide. She understood the gestures and made an affirmative motion with her hand, but Mel didn't see that. Mel pointed again to each of the beds and to each other, making himself clear, and finally, Alinta nodded, which seemed to please the new man. Mel made a grimace with his face, his teeth showing.

Mel wasn't certain how to ask if the woman needed to use the necessary, and he needed to check on the animals but didn't know how to make that clear either. The men Mel had hired for the trip had done their duty for the night, switching off while some came in to eat, but he needed to take a turn and check on the dogs and feed them too.

Mel thought the way to start was to get to know each other better. He had recognized the despair on the woman's face, seeing a resignation that had hurt his tender heart at the woman's situation. While talking over cards, Mel learned the men hadn't given any regard to the young woman's feelings when they took her from her family. Mel pointed to himself and said, "Mel Lawrence," clearly and distinctly, making sure the woman was looking at him when he did so. The aboriginal woman looked puzzled, and Mel repeated the gesture and his name. Then Mel pointed to the woman, waiting patiently as she thought about what Mel was asking. Suddenly, a light came on in her

eyes as she realized what this man wanted. She was excited, thinking Mel wanted to know her tribal affiliation, which in her mind was much more important than her personal name. Mel found the sounds too basic and guttural to pronounce when he finally heard the woman speak. Still, the woman's voice was very attractive.

Mel tried again, this time using his first name only. "Mel," he said, tapping his chest and looking expectantly at the woman, who was dressed in only a man's oversized shirt. He tapped her chest and waited patiently.

Alinta waited, realizing she had said something wrong. She felt like she had done a lot wrong around these white people. Several times, Bradley had tried to teach her to cook, but the lack of communication between them had caused her to fail. She could gather wood, but the length of chain prevented her from going too far away from his presence. She had no idea how to cook in the overly large fire the men insisted on making each night. Many times, Bradley had been disgusted as she picked up the grubs she found in the wood and popped them in her mouth. She even grabbed at grasshoppers that jumped by her and stuck them in her mouth, crunching happily on this treat and spitting out the legs and shells. She had no idea what this other man wanted. She worried her new master was going to become angry with her, and she glanced around at the many people, mostly men, watching their exchange. She wondered if this new man would share her with the other men.

"Mel," he said again, tapping his chest then tapping on the young woman's chest.

Alinta wondered at this man's persistence, then got a glimmer that perhaps he wanted her personal name. Tentatively, she said, "Alinta."

Mel smiled, showing off even and very white teeth. "Alinta," he repeated back. As the woman looked up at the large man, he said her name again, nodded, and pointed at himself, seemingly waiting for something.

Alinta thought a moment and realized the man wanted her to repeat his name. "Mel," she answered, her voice just as tentative as when she said her own name.

Mel nodded and smiled again, showing he was pleased. Alinta realized the man's grimace was a smile and answered with one of her own. Alinta released a breath she hadn't even realized she was holding and nodded, treasuring their exchange. It was the first time someone had said her name in months, and while it wasn't perfect—it didn't have the subtle range like when her mother said it— but it was something. It was hers to share, and this man had given her his name.

Mel gestured and indicated that Alinta should sit on her bed. She tensed slightly, but she obeyed. Perhaps now he would take her in full view of the other men. There were many more men than there had been before. Would he share her with them all as they had shared her mother?

Instead, Mel went over to one of the wagons, uncovered a bundle hanging off the end, and using a knife, he cut chunks of meat from the carcass. Several dogs stationed on the near side of the flock looked towards the fire and saw what Mel was doing. They waited impatiently, shifting their positions while looking towards the sheep then back towards the man. Mel took a while to fill the bucket and then covered the carcass back up with a bag. Tying it closed, he carried the bucket to one of the fires the vaqueros had kindled, not wishing to use the one that the carters had built. He skewered several of the chunks of

meat and placed them over the coals. One of the men and all three of
Carmen's boys helped turn the many chunks until they were seared
through, the fatty flesh of the mutton sizzling in the coals as it dripped.
Mel did this until all the meat was roasted, cutting the cooling chunks
into smaller pieces and tossing them back into the bucket. Then he
began to head out to the flock, stopping by each dog to portion out their
meal. Slowly, Mel made his way around the flock, making sure not to
scare the sheep but also making certain the dogs recognized his tread.
He fed all the dogs, including those owned by Carmen.

Alinta had watched, amazed, as Mel put the chain down at her feet
and cut the cooked flesh easily using one of the white man's stones her
father had coveted so. She had seen many of these stones in the camp
at various times over the months she had spent with them. Each man
seemed to own many such tools, and they didn't seem to value or prize
them as much as her people would have. She only knew she was not to
touch them. Bradley had once clouted her when she went to touch one
of their sharp edges as it shone in the hot Australian sun.

Alinta looked around, surprised that no one seemed to mind her just
sitting there on the bed the man had made. He hadn't physically
claimed her yet, but she anticipated that he would, although there was
no tent and no privacy here. That lack of privacy did not bother the
earthy woman, but she would miss the protection she felt inside the
tent. She looked across to the carter's fire and saw Bradley gazing
angrily at her as he sipped from the bottle he kept in his shirt pocket.
That was the bottle he used as a threat if she refused to eat. She
wondered if he would come to claim her back when the other white
man was done with her. She was surprised when Mel took the bucket
of meat and several others, including some boys, helped him cook the

flesh over the coals and flames. She looked at the white boys curiously. She hadn't seen children very often since she left the gathering. She'd seen white children in some of the towns they went through, but she had learned to keep her head down and not draw attention to herself while perched on her seat or in with the bags of wool as Bradley drove the wagon.

Mel ignored her and went to feed some of the odd dingo-like beasts she had noticed around the other odd bleating animals. She watched until Mel went off into the darkness then glanced back, and sure enough, Bradley was still watching her and drinking from the same bottle. She was relieved when Mel finally returned from the darkness with the bucket now filled with water he had gathered at the stream. He used it to wash his face and indicated Alinta should do the same, but no matter how many gestures he made or how often he used her personal name, she couldn't understand what he wanted. Not used to washing, and not having bathed in months to clean away the personal sweat or anything else from her body, Alinta didn't understand. Personal smell was unique to each person, and she had always felt so exposed when the rain had washed away all the sweat, dust, and layers from her body. It had left her skin feeling open and prime for the many bugs to bite in the Outback.

Mel finally gave up and went to sit with a few of the others.

"What are you going to do with her?" one of the men helping with the sheep asked from where he was sitting around one of the fires.

"Keep her," Mel grunted out, not willing to go into detail. It was none of the man's business.

Carmen glanced up at that declaration and said nothing. She too had been aware of Bradley's scrutiny since he had lost the woman at

cards. She didn't think Mel had cheated the man, but she wondered at Mel's ownership of the woman now. She'd spoken low in Spanish to Paco, giving him a word of warning that he spread to the other vaqueros. They were all ready in case trouble broke out with the carters.

Mel finally went to bed, using the ground sheet to keep off the ground and rolling up in his blanket, then indicating that Alinta should do the same. She was on the far side of the man, his larger body blocking the fires and the view of Bradley, who was still nursing his bottle and staring rudely across the fires at the aboriginal woman.

Late that night, Mel rolled over with a gun in his hand as a shadow loomed. "I suggest you go back to your fire and sleep it off mate," he suggested, the glint of the gun in his hand showing Bradley that he had been ready for him. Bradley backed off warily, surprised and alarmed at the American. It was then he realized that several of the Hispanic men also had rifles trained on him. He pretended not to see them as he made his way unsteadily back towards his tent.

Mel got up early, able to sleep after all. He was tired, but not so tired he wouldn't do his fair share of the work. He rolled up his blanket and ground sheet, smiled at Alinta, and indicated the woman should roll hers up too. Mel showed her how to roll it, so it would remain snug, then tied it off, placing Alinta's in the wagon and tying his to the back of the saddle. Together, they walked into the brush, so that they could relieve themselves. Mel was pleased that she didn't have to tell Alinta what to do as she ascertained their need for privacy. Mel turned his back as he squatted similar to Alinta, pulling down his trousers so he could take care of the necessities, then covering up his leavings with dirt using his boot. He used the paper he had brought to wipe himself

and felt a tug on the chain as Alinta used a leaf to do the same. Mel turned away, waiting for Alinta to finish and looking out at the land, so he wouldn't stare at the woman's backside. Mel was determined to find her some trousers at the next town. None of the clothes he had would fit the thin woman. For now, the oversized shirt would have to do.

Others were stirring as they returned, some heading out into the same brush to do their own morning rituals and grunting in passing. Mel gathered the horses, using his immense strength to put the pack saddles on each of them. He placed his papers in the saddlebag. Alinta watched, fascinated, and taking more of an interest in Mel's doings than she ever had in Bradley's, who had seemed to only want one of two things from her: sex and ownership. She had been surprised that the white man hadn't taken her the night before and wondered if he would be giving her back to Bradley, but he made no sign to take her back.

After a breakfast shared by the drovers and the carters, they said their goodbyes. The wagons stacked high with wool heading southeast, and the supply wagons and carts heading west and a little north, farther into the Outback, followed by the sheep and then the horses. George Granger had tried to buy some of the horses from Senora Pearson, but she wouldn't sell. Backed up by the guns of her very capable looking vaqueros, he wasn't about to argue with the woman. She wished him well and on his way before being helped into the saddle of her mighty stallion and heading off after her other horses.

Alinta had been surprised when Mel brought her a plate and encouraged her to eat. The woman kept glancing back at Bradley and the other carters she was familiar with. Strangely, this morning, she

was hungry, and she ate what Mel brought her. When she was finished, Mel showed her how to wash up from the bucket, and while she didn't do a very good job, wiping her fingers on her shirt instead, she understood a little more of what this man was trying to get her to do. After making sure all the packs on his horses were tight, Mel signaled to Alinta to come closer, and to her surprise, she was lifted into one of this man's wagons. Mel handed her the length of chain that was attached to her neck. She glanced from the big man back to Bradley, who still wore a sullen look on his face, his bleary eyes glaring at the aboriginal woman and the large white man. She realized that this white man owned her now.

George Granger shook his head, watching Mel Lawrence leading his packhorses with the woman now in one of his wagons and holding her own chain. He knew Bradley was angry about her loss, but no one had made him gamble her away. He'd lost a terrific amount of money, but no one had forced him to keep playing. He suspected that Mel Lawrence had somehow cheated the man, but there was no proof since Bradley had also won several hands.

Alinta watched the big, white man, wondering about him as the wagon lurched and dipped along on the track. He held onto a long line of those odd animals that had packs tied to them. Occasionally, he looked at Alinta, saw her watching him, and smiled while nodding to her. Later, he handed off the rope to someone else to lead the animals

and went to help with the odd baaing animals that were creating so much dust.

Her mother had once explained that there were Creators that brought all people into being and that the elders kept the sacred stories for them. She also explained that the first time a mother felt a baby move in her womb, the animal she saw first would be its totem and be part of its life forever; its personality intertwined in the animal's spirit. Alinta wondered what her totem spirit was. She hadn't received her totem in the tribe and been told special stories that would help her become the woman she was meant to be. She wondered if her baby would be affected by this. She knew she had seen a hawk the day her baby moved, and she was convinced that he or she would have excellent, far-reaching eyesight and would be fierce. She wondered often if her own lack of a totem would affect her child's totem and make it weaker. Today, she felt her baby moving again after she had been gazing at the big white man. She attributed something to that but didn't fully understand it yet. Something about this new man, this Mel, was part of her child's destiny. She fervently wished she had an elder to ask.

CHAPTER SIX

At the next town, Mel inquired where they might find a blacksmith to remove the chains from the younger woman. Several people looked at this man disapprovingly, but as he wasn't holding the chains, they shrugged, and someone finally gave him the information he was asking for. Word spread that a large flock of Merino sheep was being held outside of town along with some of the most beautiful horses anyone had ever seen. Some people hiked to see the sight. Seeing such fine sheep and horses being taken into the Outback would provide gossip for many years to come. The name Twin Station meant nothing to any of them, but now, they had a name when they talked about it.

Alinta didn't understand that the man was going to remove the collar or ankle chain, and Mel had to hold her down as the man used brute strength to pound out the pins holding them together. Only when

Mel let her go and opened the collar around her neck did she understand that her new man was having it removed. The wool that had been wadded under the iron to keep her from chaffing fell to the ground. She rubbed where it had been, wondering if Mel would have another put on. She immediately felt the loss of weight from the heavy iron around her neck, which despite the wool, had chaffed her skin. Then Mel had the chains around her ankles removed. She watched as Mel talked with the very strong but dirty man who had pounded out the white man's stone, and they appeared to work out a deal with Mel leaving the collar and chains behind. Alinta didn't know it, but the iron could be melted down and used again, and the blacksmith valued it.

Mel watched the woman, wondering if she understood she was free. She followed Mel unquestioningly, but then, she didn't speak the language. Mel went into a store, and Alinta was immediately intimidated by all the unfamiliar sights and smells. Everything reeked of the white man. She had no comprehension of any of it, and she stood as close to Mel as she could. She could see others looking at her, frowning at her, and she didn't understand that either. She didn't understand what she had done wrong that they would frown at her so.

Alinta stood still as Mel held the white man's clothing up against her body, wondering what he was doing. Mel purchased ready-made shirts as well as miner's pants and underwear. Alinta smiled for the first time when Mel tried hats on her head, looking up at them in wonder, her eyes almost rolling back as she tried to see them since they covered her eyes at first. One by one, Mel tried hats on the smaller woman's head until she found one that fit. It was Carmen who found it and handed it to the man to try it on the Aborigine. Alinta wasn't aware it was a child's stockman's hat, but she liked it and was pleased

when Mel smiled at the fit and left it on her head. Carmen smiled too, seeing the woman's delight over the small hat. After paying for his purchases, Mel gestured, and Alinta followed him out of the store. As they headed back to the camp outside of town, Alinta had to trot to keep up with the taller man's long strides. Her legs felt very different without the weight of the chains on them and slowing her down.

Mel allowed Alinta other freedoms as well. Her gathering stick had been lost when she was captured, and Alinta searched among the deadfalls for another that she could fashion using stones to smooth it. Mel watched, wishing she could ask the Aborigine what she was doing. Still, the word game, as he termed it, was coming along, and Alinta had a phenomenal memory. Mel was pleased when Carmen and her children joined in on the game, teaching the aboriginal woman many words he hadn't thought to teach her. Alinta remembered all the words she had acquired, only having to repeat them two or three times before they were hers. Mel was surprised that the woman had no words for dog or horse in her language. Apparently, they didn't have these animals where the Aborigine came from. The closest she came to dog was dingo, and that seemed universal. The wild dogs were usually heard at night as they trailed their large flock for a time, but the combination of man's scent and dogs seemed to be a deterrent. However, they were traveling and coming into other territories where more of the wild dogs existed, and these new dogs tried their patience by attempting to make a meal of their sheep.

Alinta took an interest in their cooking under Mel's tutelage. She was amazed at the bounty in their wagons. The rice and peas were a favorite of hers, but she didn't really like the fat from the mutton, preferring the meat to be nearly raw rather than well done. Salt pork was a taste that left her in awe, and beef was her favorite meat. She searched for and found seeds and other things off the trail as Mel allowed her to roam. She watched as Mel cooked meat for the dogs nightly, and when Mel offered to show her how to do this chore, she learned quickly, helping with this messy and disagreeable job when she realized Mel wanted her to.

"She'll have to go eventually, won't she?" Carmen asked as they rode their horses at the front of the column, the dust that the sheep kicked up on the track too much to ride drag too often.

"I hope she will be happy to be returned to her family," Mel said, watching the Aborigine effortlessly club a lizard and put it into the bag she had given her. Alinta had been amazed at the fine bag. It was much finer than any she could have woven from spinifex. She had turned it over and over after Mel gave it to her, examining it closely.

"You think they will want her back?" Carmen knowingly asked.

"I have no idea. That's one thing I hope to ask her as she learns English." Mel did worry. The woman, more a girl, seemed cheerful, well-meaning, and bright. Did she want to go back to her family? There were many things Mel wanted to ask her, but the language barrier was only a part of their problem. The woman didn't seem to have what Mel would have termed common sense. She didn't seem to understand that things could be broken, that not everything was made of iron, and Alinta had cringed in terror when she accidentally broke a bottle and their cook, one of Carmen's men, had started yelling at her in consternation over the broken glass. The pretty phrases in Spanish had sounded musical, but the cook's tone had frightened the wild woman.

"Easy there, easy. It can be replaced, right, Jose?" Mel asked as he came running up, and Alinta cowered, expecting a blow to fall. He

pulled the girl up into his arms, towering over her by at least a foot, and his heart went out to the terrified girl.

"Si, si," he said contritely, having sworn because he was upset over the mess of glass in his carefully prepared food. He began shoveling it into the fire. After all, no one could eat food that had glass in it. "I am sorry, Alinta," he said, trying to touch her on the arm, but she cringed away. His face told how sorry he was as he watched her.

Alinta might not understand the words, but the tone told a lot more, and his body language gave away a lot more than he intended. She looked at him wonderingly, understanding him as little clues gave her ideas about what was being said. She realized that Mel was holding her but not so hard that she couldn't get away if she wanted. She looked up at the big man in as much wonder as she had looked at Jose. Realizing no one was angry at her, and no one was going to strike her, she relaxed. The concern she heard in Mel's voice towards the man named Jose helped her begin to fit these things together in her mind. Things had changed a lot for this primitive woman, and she was trying to figure out these new white people.

Alinta could see that Mel and Carmen were vastly different white people, and although the Hispanic people were dark too—and getting darker from the hot Australian sun—they were still a lot lighter than her own people. She didn't think of them as Hispanic because that hadn't been explained to her, but at the same time, she wouldn't have understood it yet. Mel was obviously one of those white men but was nothing like the white men who had captured her. His kindness alone intrigued the aboriginal woman.

"Did Alinta do something bad?" Rachel, Carmen's young daughter, asked worriedly as she came running up.

"No, it was an accident," Mel explained to the little girl, his voice softening.

Alinta was fascinated by Carmen's children, not having seen white children up close before. The white children she had seen in the towns they had gone through never came near the wild woman. The offer of friendship between the town's children and Carmen's children was temporary, for an evening if they were near enough to a town or station that happened to have children, but it was immediately accepted, and Alinta watched avidly as they played together. Remembering her own childhood that seemed so long ago, she wondered at the child growing inside of her. She was aware of it now, even if her belly had only a slight bulge.

Alinta left the safety of Mel's arms to help Jose. He was at first surprised by her attempts to help him clean up, then she cut herself on the glass, not understanding that it was sharp, and the shards were dangerous.

"She's bleeding! Alinta's bleeding!" Rachel announced on seeing the blood.

Alinta put her thumb wonderingly in her mouth. She tasted the food, the dirt, and the blood on it, then immediately spit it out.

Mel gently pulled the thumb out of her mouth and handed her a handkerchief, showing her how to wrap it around the bleeding appendage. The red color of the material seemed to fascinate the woman, and she stared at it. Mel applied pressure, amused at the primitive woman's fascination and wondering what would happen to her when they parted ways. He too had noticed the rounding belly and knew it wasn't just from their good food. At first, he had wondered if it was from starvation, but then common sense had told him that Bradley

must have impregnated the poor woman. He felt almost paternal towards the young woman, but at the same time, he knew he cared for her and worried what would happen when they found more aboriginal people and she went with them.

CHAPTER SEVEN

They continued traveling. Alinta had been surprised when Mel asked rather than telling her to ride in the wagon, but it had also confused her. She had perfectly good legs, and for the most part, she preferred to walk, so she could gather things. She had never considered riding in anything before, mostly because she had never seen a wagon, a cart, or a horse before she'd been captured.

As they made their way west, Alinta noticed that the weather was getting hotter and hotter. Watching the others, she could see they weren't used to the heat. It didn't bother her in the least, but occasionally, she wished to take off the shirt Mel had provided her with. She had several now, all carefully rolled away in the bedroll Mel had given her to use. Alinta didn't understand the concept of ownership and didn't consider that any of these things belonged to her.

In her mind, they were simply things that Mel had asked her to use or transport. She diligently rolled them up daily as they got underway, and she changed the shirt every few days as Mel had explained to her. She didn't understand about washing out the soiled or dirty clothes until Mel showed her. She really liked her hat because it helped to fan away the pesky flies that were so prevalent in the Outback. She liked how the shadows played as she wore the hat on her head. She saw that everyone had a hat, even the children, and she wore hers proudly.

They returned to one of the towns Alinta had passed through with the other group of men. The ferry was there again, something Alinta didn't understand the first time, and she had been terrified when the wagon had been pushed onto the floating platform with her on it. The water under it unnerved her. She would have preferred to try to cross under her own legs, but could see it was deep enough, dirty enough, and wide enough that she might have had difficulty. She thought she heard them refer to this place as Menindee, and then Mel confirmed that, pointing at the town and repeating the word until Alinta tried it hesitantly. Her knowledge of their words was increasing. She listened at night, not understanding most of the stories they told but catching a familiar word here and there. She wasn't confident enough to ask Mel what some words meant, but she continued to listen and observe, her dark eyes darting about all the time in wonderment.

The furry animals, sheep Mel called them, went across the wooden platform to the other side of the river first, then the platform came back and they rolled on the wagons and carts. It took many trips to get them across as there were so many sheep. Alinta overheard Mel talking to Carmen.

"Someday, they will have steel rails to towns such as this," Mel commented, looking back as the town receded across the river.

"I hope it doesn't ruin the land," Carmen agreed as she imagined it.

Alinta wondered what steel rails meant. She knew that the collar she had worn was iron since Mel had given her that word, but she also used the word steel for the white man's stone sometimes. It was very confusing.

Alinta liked the days when they stopped to let the sheep graze, every three days or so. It gave her time to scavenge and collect seeds and fruits that the white people didn't seem to understand. She shared them with Mel when he was willing, but the bugs, grubs, lizards, and snakes were of no interest to anyone but Alinta. This bounty was not only delicious to the woman but added to the white man's food, which was helping her put on weight that her baby desperately needed.

Alinta became depressed as they approached the areas where she had last seen her parents and brother. She had hoped to find some sign of them. She was certain she had found their last camping spot, but it had been too long, and the weather had erased any signs of them being there. They continued down the endless track west, and she was far from her tribes' hunting grounds. Even if she could find her way there, she knew she could never go back. She knew they wouldn't welcome her.

Alinta watched Mel, who treated her differently than the men from before. Mel was so nice to her. She knew all she could do was learn his ways and hope he would want to keep her. She was also beginning to realize that Mel was maybe not what he seemed. In fact, she was certain that Mel wasn't a man at all. Her tribe, in fact, all tribes, had revered people like this, who had a spirit living inside them of the opposite sex. She understood this, and it didn't bother her. She didn't discuss it with Mel, but only because Mel didn't say anything about it. There was also the language barrier, and while she was with Bradley, she hadn't bothered to learn any words in their language. With Mel, who not only encouraged her but helped her to learn the words, she was feeling the need to communicate with the white man.

Alinta watched as Carmen's children rode horses. These animals were fascinating to her. She found them beautiful but was afraid to approach too closely, even when Mel asked if she wanted to ride. She preferred to be far from them in the back of the wagon when she did ride, but the next wagon was right behind her and was also being pulled by horses or oxen, another word she had trouble trying to pronounce. The children seemed unafraid of these horses, relishing the opportunity to ride them at every opportunity. She could see very clearly that these were not some weird aberration of horse-child or horse-man as her family had all thought when they first saw them long ago.

Mel tried to convince Alinta to wear boots or shoes, trying several different sizes on her small feet, even shoes the children wore, but the Aborigine didn't understand the concept. Mel finally realized the soles of the woman's feet were as hard as any leather she could put on them to protect them, but when Alinta got a thorn in her foot one day, she made her ride in the wagon for a few days after it was extracted. Alinta was soon back to walking beside the long column, collecting her seeds, fruits, and various bugs that Mel found unappealing. The wild fruits, vegetables, and seeds had been a delicious addition to the rice and peas they ate with the mutton that was so readily available. One of the men pointed out that the natural fruits were a good way to ward off scurvy, but at first, Alinta didn't understand when Mel and several others

encouraged her to find more fruits for the entire party. Once it was clear that she was being asked to find more of these fruits, she was delighted she could help. Mel smiled to see her in the long shirt, proudly wearing her child-sized stockmen's hat and collecting fruit in the sack Mel had provided. Her needs, wants, and desires were simple.

CHAPTER EIGHT

Alinta watched as strangers approached Mel on horses. It was a man and a woman, and as they rode up, Carmen went out to meet them. She watched them interact, unable to hear their conversation over the noises of the wagons and the many animals behind their long train. She finally heard that they were Harold and Fabiola, and Carmen seemed happy to see them.

As they came over the top of a rise, Alinta could see a little valley and many more of the white man's structures they had seen on the trip. It was like a little town. She was surprised to see an Aborigine village on one side. Familiar with the shapes of their huts and the color of their skin, she wondered at them living so close to white men. She watched as the men in their party herded the large flock of sheep into wooden structures helped by the dogs. Mel told her the wooden structures were called pens. The horses and oxen were herded into other pens, and the dogs were kept away once all the animals were in their pens.

Carmen directed Mel and Alinta to one of the structures. The primitive woman was curious because it wasn't at all like the store she had been inside so long ago. There was a porch, and Mel enunciated that word, so Alinta would get it. It was broad and shady with vines crawling up the wooden support posts. Inside was a living room, another couple of words that Alinta didn't understand. Aboriginal people didn't have living rooms, nor did they have kitchens or bedrooms. It fascinated Alinta when Mel showed her a bed. She didn't understand what a bed was used for until Mel lay on it and patted the bed beside her. These white people seemed to have a lot of *things* that they didn't need to make. Sleeping with a rolled-up blanket on the ground was good enough. Still, she would oblige Mel, who asked instead of ordering her about. Alinta wanted to please Mel.

Wagons pulled up at the house next door, and Mel went over to help unload Carmen's things. There was too much for the house, and the rest of the things were taken to a barn. Barn, that was also a word and a concept that Alinta didn't understand. They seemed to use that same word for both structures that held animals and things. They also used the word shed sometimes, and this confused Alinta even more.

She watched only, as Mel wouldn't let her help carry things into the house or the barn, then she watched as the men filled the carts and wagons with great big bales. They were the same things Bradley and the other men had been hauling. To see them loading those up brought back bad memories, and she was grateful she wasn't expected to help with this chore or go near the men doing the work.

"I need you to stay here in the house," Mel explained to her that night. They had brought Mel's things into the living room, and she was sorting through them. They both heard the dogs settling down for the night under the house. Mel and Alinta had just finished feeding them. The dogs had nothing to do now that the sheep were in the pens.

"I no go with Mel?" she asked, hurt and wondering why Mel was leaving her in this house. She looked around, wondering what she had done wrong that would make Mel leave her alone here.

"No, I'm just going away for a few days," she tried to explain, knowing the simple woman didn't understand. Then she got an idea. "You watch my things?" she asked, gesturing to the many pack saddles and other things she had pulled from the wagons and stacked in the front room.

Alinta grasped that immediately, proud that Mel would ask her to guard her property. She took pride in that responsibility. Mel explained she could get food at the kitchens but might want to cook it here. She showed her how to start a fire in the stove but cooking on the stove was too much for the woman to grasp. Mel also showed Alinta where to fetch the meat to feed the dogs.

Alinta watched as Mel rode away with Carmen and Fabiola the next day, wondering at the white man's ability to handle those animals they called horses. She saw that women could do it too and wondered if she would ever get over her awe of the large animals.

Alita ended up making a fire out behind the house in a ring, cooking mutton, damper, rice, and peas for her meal before giving the dogs meat for their food. The dogs watched the nearly feral woman warily. They had not interacted with her much, but Mel had ordered them to stay, and they would obey. Each dog had come out and squatted or lifted its leg, but now, the feces were building up, and the flies were terrible. One of the Aborigines came. Although he was unable to speak Alinta's tribes' language, she showed Alinta with pantomiming what a shovel was for and how to bury the feces or throw them farther away from the home paddock. Alinta understood and took her duty seriously.

Another of the villagers came by to try and talk to Alinta, but she didn't speak their language either, and they looked curiously at each other, noting the differences that indicated they were from different tribes.

Alinta was curiously relieved to see Mel return a few days later.

"How are you feeling?" Mel asked upon seeing the pregnant woman.

"Fine," she admitted, one of the few words she truly knew the meaning of, although she had learned a lot.

"Baby making you sick?" she asked, concerned but hoping that the woman had rested. Mel saw how neat and orderly the supplies were in the house and wondered how hard she had worked. Mel had made it clear weeks ago on their long trip out here that she understood Alinta was with child.

"Baby fine," she said, rubbing her rounding belly.

"Good, good," Mel said, nodding.

Mel arranged for another couple of villagers to come and try to talk with Alinta. Although they didn't speak her language, using pantomime, they were able to ask if she wished to stay with Mel or go back to her own people.

Alinta made it clear she didn't want to go back, and her people wouldn't want her. "Mr. Mel no want me?" she asked.

"I want you," Mel stated clearly, then said, "If you want to go with me, you can. If you want to go back to your family, you can. If you want to stay here, you can. It's your decision." She understood Alinta's hesitation now as she tried to make herself understood.

"Alinta's decision?"

Mel nodded, smiling encouragingly.

"I go you?"

"Only if you want, but I'll be roaming, and that won't be good for your baby," she told her.

"You want Alinta go you?" she asked, and the Aborigine, who was trying to help, gestured some more, making himself understood. Here in the white man's station, the men were to be obeyed, and he was getting exasperated with the white Yank giving the young woman a choice. Did she not understand how big a decision that was for the young girl?

"Yes, but only if Alinta wants to go with me," Mel responded.

"Alinta want go Mel," she said imperfectly, looking relieved.

Mel smiled, nodding, and Harold, who had watched, amused, nodded to the aboriginal elder, who had tried to interpret for them. Mel wasn't sure he had helped, but she wasn't sure he hadn't helped either. Mel thanked him, and Harold sent him on his way.

"So, you are going to take the woman as your own?" he asked in an almost insinuating tone.

"No, she isn't my own," Mel objected. "She is my friend, and she's welcome to come with me while I search for a place of my own. She was born here, but I feel as though I belong too. Maybe we can find a place together."

CHAPTER NINE

Alinta watched as Mel took her horses to a man working with the white man's stone, iron they called it. It still bothered her to watch, and she unconsciously rubbed her neck in remembrance of the collar she had once worn. The big, beefy man was putting metal on the bottoms of the horse's feet. It smelled terrible as the white man's stone caused a burning smell to rise from them. Alinta didn't understand when Mel called them shoes because she had also called those leather things she wanted Alinta to wear by the same word, but Alinta nodded and tried to sound the word.

Next, Alinta watched as Mel packed and repacked the supplies she had kept so neatly for her. She worried that she had done something wrong, but Mel didn't say anything to her. Mel seemed restless as she waited, and Alinta wondered why they were waiting here in this house.

The dogs under the house were restless too. When Carmen and Fabiola returned, she saw that Mel was relieved. As they ate dinner together, she once again tried to use the fork the way Mel had shown her. She preferred her fingers but saw that was frowned upon, so she would try for Mel's sake. She wanted the woman to be proud of her. She was eager to please Mel in return for rescuing her from Bradley. At dinner they discussed things that Alinta did not understand about where she would be going. She had no concept of words like 'south' or 'north' and only caught a couple words she understood. She understood the word Cobdogla but only because she recognized their attempts to say an Aborigine word.

The next day, Mel spent a lot of time with the other men and the dogs. They were doing something with the sheep. Some went in one pen, others into another pen. Alinta didn't understand it, but it was fascinating to watch the commotion. The sheep stirred up a lot of dust, and she tried to stay upwind of it, so it wasn't blowing in her face as she watched them work and tried to understand what they were doing.

The following day, she was surprised when Mel hoisted her onto one of the horses and handed her the lead ropes to the other horses that were loaded with the many packs Mel had sorted. She was proud that Mel trusted her with this important task. Alinta had no idea that her horse was following Mel's because it chose to and not because of anything she did to control it. Mel, her dingo-like dogs, Carmen, Fabiola, and several of the men Alinta had heard were called vaqueros helped push the sheep along. It looked like a lot, but not nearly as many had come along the track from so far away. At least half were headed north, although Alinta didn't grasp the concept of this direction. She only knew that her horse followed Mel, and she kept going when

the large woman veered off to check the flock for strays when a dog didn't do it for her.

They traveled like this for a couple days, approaching an odd set of domed hills. On the far side the sheep slowed to graze, and Alinta watched as Fabiola, Carmen, and the other men left them. She was feeling slightly ill from the motion of the horse, but she wouldn't stop helping Mel because she knew it must be important. Mel seemed to keep the sheep at a slower pace, which helped her nausea. Mel helped Alinta down from the horse for their noon break to eat and rest and again when they made camp at night. Mel also taught her more *English* words. She now understood that the language the whites spoke was called English. She learned words like saltbrush and mallee seed, also giving Mel words in her own language if she knew the plant. She liked the word billabong, but Mel also called it a spring. These kinds of double words confused her, but she didn't stop learning their many words.

Mel showed her how to hobble the horses, explaining it was so they couldn't wander too far away from their camp. As they gathered wood, Alinta was delighted to use her walking stick to turn over some of the wood and find grubs. Mel was delighted when Alinta helped weave branches to make a hut. For her it was simple to weave it so it would shed the rain. For once, Alinta became the teacher, and she beamed with delight as Mel praised her and thanked her. She wasn't used to the concept of thanks but was learning it was important to the white man.

Mel made more of a concerted effort to show Alinta how to cook, and Alinta was pleased. She wanted to learn how to make the white man's food but hadn't liked it when there had been so many people watching her. Now, it was just the two of them, and she was much

more willing and eager to please her rescuer. Mel allowed her to regularly use one of the sharp white man's stones, a knife he called it. It amazed her that it was sharper than the stones she had chipped over the years. No wonder her father had coveted the metal. She had learned it was not stone, although she still thought of it as the white man's stone. It was called metal, and that was the word she would use from then on. They cut mutton, not only for their own consumption but also for the many dogs that accompanied their large flock of sheep. When Mel had shown her how to cover up the carcass to keep the flies out, Alinta nodded wisely. Then, Mel presented her with a knife of her own including a sheath to keep it in. Alinta was surprised that Mel would give her such riches.

She was also fascinated by the sharpness of the metal. It always seemed to stay sharp, but she had seen Mel sharpen hers on something she called a whetstone. It sounded close enough to the words 'white man's stone' that Alinta could make the comparison. "Careful there," Mel cautioned her as she tested the blade.

The meat, the rice and peas, and the spongy bread that they called damper, were cooked in what they called pots or the wider ones they called pans. Again, the valuable metals were shaped into useful things that the Aborigine stared at in wonder. These white people were clever, and their tools were way beyond anything her people had. No wonder people had coveted them. Standing up, she stretched to help her aching back and heard Mel gasp. Alinta looked around, wondering if she had missed seeing something. Alinta knew she sensed things way before the white woman did, but when she didn't see anything that might have caused Mel's dismay, she dismissed it.

After dinner she helped clean those pots, pans, and plates. She put them out on rocks to dry as Mel had showed her. Stretching again when she was finished, she felt the baby bump as she looked about thoughtfully. She was so pleased to be here alone with Mel. She thought about when Mel had the Aborigines talk to her, making it clear that she had the choice to go with Mel or not. She herself didn't understand the other Aborigines' language, and when she thought Mel didn't want her to go with her, she had been panicked. Finally, she was appeased when she realized Mel did want her. It had never occurred to her that Mel was giving her a choice. She didn't understand that it was *her* choice. She had hoped that Mel would be her mate once she was far from Bradley and men like him. She would do everything in her power to be the best mate to Mel she could be. She'd learn everything that Mel would teach her, and perhaps someday, Mel would tell her that she wanted her to be her mate. In the meantime, she would show she was willing to do whatever Mel wanted of her. For now, that consisted of learning to cook and any other tasks she wanted her to do.

She watched as Mel took her firing sticks—guns she called them—and walked around the temporary fold she had made using sticks with rope strung between them. Mel had explained that it wouldn't really hold the animals, but they thought it did. Alinta wondered how Mel knew what the animals were thinking.

As Mel relaxed by the fire, she smoked from a pipe. Alinta knew what these things were since some of her people did the same, mostly the elders. Mel cut a notch in a stick she kept, explaining it was to help keep the date. Alinta nodded but didn't understand what that meant. If it was cold, you shivered or put on more skins, and if it was hot, you took the extra skins off. She knew white people used clothes, not skins, but the concept was the same. If it was dark, you slept, and if it was light, you worked or moved. She didn't understand the concept of days or dates.

She watched as Mel disrobed, taking off her boots, which were like shoes but longer. These boots went to Mel's knees. Then she removed her pants and below them there was what she called summer underwear. Alinta wondered why the summer would need underwear but had accepted the words. Mel's long shirt, not much different than the ones Mel had provided Alinta, hung down to her thighs, although they were longer on Alinta, hanging down to her calves just like a dress.

That night, Alinta sensed a tension in the air between them. She was aware that Mel had stared at her frequently that night. She wondered if she had done something wrong but didn't think she had because Mel hadn't become angry while explaining things she wanted Alinta to learn. Alinta wondered what it would be like to be held by the big and strong Mel. The woman had held her at various times on this trip, but Alinta craved it now. While thinking about being held by Mel, Alinta fell into a dreamless sleep.

CHAPTER TEN

Alinta woke as soon as Mel started to move around. After getting dressed, she hurried to start their breakfast, and while that was cooking, Alinta went off into the brush, out of the way to take care of her necessities. The damper was heated by the time she returned, and she fried some of the leftover meat from dinner the night before.

She watched as Mel walked around the sheep. The sky got lighter, but it was overcast with ominous rain clouds. The dogs stirred and greeted Mel, and she talked to them, praising them for watching the sheep. There were more of them than Mel had kept under the house back at Carmen and Fabiola's station, and they had come along the trail with them. As Alinta watched, when Mel got to the far side, she unlimbered the fire stick and shot, then she shot again. The noise was loud in the still air of the morning. Alinta could hear the yelping of a dingo. The sheep surged slightly, but the dogs held them at bay. The sound of the gun scared Alinta too. She didn't go anywhere near the guns that Mel kept.

Alinta hurried to finish preparing breakfast for them, placing the food on tin plates with a fork and a knife. After breakfast, she washed the dishes in water and laid them out to dry.

Mel let the sheep out into the large field near their camp and left the dogs to watch them as he began to haul deadfalls from the woods and chop down any dead trees. Alinta rushed to help, but Mel wouldn't let her lift any of the heavier trees, explaining that it would be too hard on her baby. Alinta was able to help dig up some of the plants that Mel indicated she wanted to replant around the large fold she was building. Alinta didn't quite understand what a fold was, having only seen the rope ones, but she got the idea as it took shape, remembering the pens back on the other station. The walls were rising through a combination of dead trees, split rails, and plants. Although Mel wouldn't let her lift anything heavy, she found she could weave sticks, smaller trees, and plants between the rails that Mel was raising, and Mel was pleased with this help.

Alinta made lunch, tiffin she was told it was called. This was another dual word that confused the woman. Explaining that lunch was American, and tiffin was Australian, meant nothing to the aboriginal woman. Mel's smiles showed she didn't mind the woman's confusion and didn't mean any harm by laughter. Alinta just accepted these odd differences, adding to her vocabulary daily.

That night, Alinta heard the dingoes, and Mel was ready. She killed another one. Mel seemed tired and irritable as she worked hard to finish more of the permanent fold they were building. Over the next

few days, they continued to bring wood, Mel chopping down whole trees and Alinta moving plants until it was a sturdily constructed fold. Mel seemed relieved when it was built, herding the flock into it and taking her dirty clothes to a billabong to wash. Mel got in but despite her best efforts, she was unable to entice Alinta to join her. She couldn't convince the young woman to immerse herself in the waters of the pond. She did eventually convince her to change into a clean shirt-dress, so the one she was wearing could be washed. Later, she would convince Alinta to wear drawers and eventually, pants, but only after the weather turned colder and the rain finally came. With the colder weather, Alinta realized that having additional clothes on made her warmer.

The dingoes continued their efforts to get at the sheep despite the sturdy, new fold. Mel took Alinta and a couple of the dogs along with her to hunt them. Once Alinta realized that Mel wanted the den, she tracked them back to it easily. The holes were nearly invisible against the dusky dirt around the rocks where they had dug. Knowing the dingoes would be back from hunting in the morning, Mel piled stones up around all the holes she could find. The dogs were eager to dig at the holes, whining and smelling their nemeses, but Mel commanded them away. She and Alinta gathered wood and dried grass. They left them near the holes but not so near that the human smell would distract the wild dogs.

Early the next morning, leaving the hungry sheep in the fold, they hurried with several of the dogs back to the den and filled the higher holes with the rocks, then started a fire with the wood and grasses and pushed them in the lower holes. Remembering the stockman's tale of how he had done this, Mel tried to duplicate his efforts, and this proved

to be successful. The dingoes, tired from a night of hunting, tried to get out of their holes, but the rocks were too heavy, and they were suffocated in their den. The dogs were agitated and would have dug the dingoes out to fight them, but Mel kept them away, and none of the dingoes in this den escaped.

The threat was now eliminated, and Mel strengthened the fold while the sheep were out of it during the day. This fold was large and could hold the entire flock. During the day when she was out, she scouted around, going farther and farther afield until she found a place where she wanted to build another permanent fold. The sheep were again hunted by dingoes in the new location, but Mel was a good shot, and Alinta was so in tune with nature that she spotted them long before the dogs. Now that Alinta understood Mel wanted to kill the dingoes, she would spot them and point them out to Mel. They eliminated another smaller den. This one had pups in it by the sounds they heard coming out of it. Mel was sad at the thought of killing the young, but the young would grow up and begin hunting, and she couldn't afford to have them around the sheep she intended to raise on these acres. Alinta, listening as Mel explained this to her, was surprised that Mel would hunt these dingoes and then be sad that she had to kill their young. She was thoughtful as she tried to understand these odd white people's ways.

A few showers fell as they built the folds, but it wasn't until they were done building the third fold that the rain came in earnest. The creeks rose and the rivers overflowed. Entire areas that were normally quite dry were flooded out. Alinta recognized the signs of ancient floods and always led her horse and the packhorses to higher ground where they could make their huts. Some days, they were miserable as

it rained, and the sheep cropped the grass despite the wet. Mel explained her worry about disease and even the cold for the poor sodden sheep. One of the sheep was lost to a snake bite, another to some plants it ate along a creek where they had stopped, and still others were lost to dingoes.

They moved on despite the rains. Mel made sure they always crossed a creek or river before they settled on higher ground for the night. She explained that it was a good practice because you never knew what rain was coming down from upstream. Alinta understood this because her English had improved, and she was no longer thinking in the aboriginal language. After all this time spent in the constant presence of Mel, she now thought in English. She liked that Mel took the time to explain things to her, even if she didn't always understand everything. She didn't ask questions, but Mel sometimes saw that she didn't understand a concept and explained further, talking to hear herself talk.

The wild animals fascinated Mel, and she watched them while talking to Alinta. She was trying to know her language but was mainly teaching her the names of things she knew in English. The words kangaroo or wallaby were easy, even cockatoo or bird, but Mel didn't know some of the animals and had no one to ask. The teaching wasn't always one-sided. One time, Alinta warned Mel about a snake, the worm-like twitching of its tail the only thing visible in the leaves as it tried to entice its prey, then sprang out to strike and kill whatever dared come near. Alinta sensed it and threw pebbles until it sprang up, attacking, and then slithered off. Mel was amazed when her friend showed her things like this.

Alinta was astonished that Mel didn't know what seemed like such ordinary things to her, and she was pleased to teach her what she knew. The white man/woman had so many wondrous things and seemed to know so much, but Alinta could still show her things that her parents had shown her long ago.

Despite the rain, Mel slowly got the fourth fold built. She was really honing her skills with the axe, and her arm muscles were building up. Alinta admired the body she occasionally saw, although it was usually covered up with clothes. Alinta's scavenged plants and fruits added to their diet and helped to stretch their meager supplies. She even convinced Mel to shoot a kangaroo. It was delicious, a nice change from mutton, and Alinta prepared several of their meals with the meat.

Mel had taken the skins of the wethers they had butchered for food and stretched them on the roofs of their shelters to dry and scrape the fat from them. This was something Alinta was happy to help with as it didn't require anything but the use of her hands, arms, and shoulders. She learned from Mel to rub the skins with something she called peppermint, which she got from certain trees. It gave the pelts a nice smell. Next, Mel showed Alinta, who was fascinated with the needle, how to stitch the hides together. Mel's first project was a stockman's coat made from warm wool that would keep out the elements. When she made a much smaller version for Alinta, the woman refused to wear it at first. It was heavy, and the Aborigine was unused to carrying such weight. When Mel finally convinced Alinta to wear it for warmth, she used it both as a coat and as a blanket. Not only were the coats warm but they were rainproof, and Alinta learned to appreciate hers.

Alinta noticed the dogs' reactions, and she tensed up, sensing danger. When she recognized Carmen, Fabiola, several stockmen, and the vaqueros approaching their camp, she relaxed. It had been hard to peer through the driving rain, but she recognized the two women and watched as Mel greeted them.

"Hello, Alinta," the two women greeted the aboriginal woman, noting how pregnant she looked as she sat sideways on her horse while watching the sheep and wearing her sheepskin coat.

"Misses Carmen, Misses Fabiola," she said in reply, having trouble with the second name as it didn't come easy to her. She'd practiced as Mel had talked often and admiringly about these two women.

"Alinta would you mind showing the men where to put our supplies in the hut?" Mel asked her, making it her choice, but the eager young woman immediately set off on her horse with a couple of the men following behind her pulling the packhorses.

They unloaded the heavily laden packhorses into the bark hut Mel and Alinta had built for this campsite. The men wouldn't let her carry anything but a light package or two. They avoided looking at her heavily pregnant stomach.

Alinta was not aware of the conversation that occurred after she left the sheep.

"She's gotten so big," Carmen commented when the pregnant woman was out of earshot.

Mel nodded. "I estimate she's due right after the sheep."

"That sounds like a lot of work," Fabiola mentioned, wondering how Mel was going to cope. She knew she wouldn't want to have a flock this big and a pregnant woman to worry about.

"And two of my bitches are pregnant too," Mel lamented with a laugh at her situation. It was of her own making. She should have delayed letting the rams in among her sheep until later, but there was nothing she could have done about Alinta's due date. They were only guessing anyway, having no idea when the carter had impregnated the poor woman.

Carmen laughed with her, and after a moment, Fabiola joined in. "Do you want me to send some of my men to help?" Carmen asked helpfully.

"You'll have enough to tend to with your own flocks. I knew what the work entailed before I set off on this adventure," Mel reminded her well-meaning friend.

"I'm sure you did," she consoled. "If you need—" she began, but Mel cut her off.

"Thank you."

"Damned independent cuss. We could send a couple—" Fabiola began again exasperatedly.

"I know," Mel returned, sounding just as exasperated.

Carmen shook her head but laughed, so Fabiola wouldn't get angry. She knew Mel was independent, headstrong, and probably out to prove a point. Still, the land she had chosen was beautiful. It had taken them a while to find her, following the path the sheep had taken as they grazed and finding the well-made folds.

Both women were glad to help bring in the flock of sheep to the nearly finished fold that Mel had been building despite the winter rains.

The rope stretched across on two sides, but the sheep were relatively safe. Dinner was a grand affair, and they continued talking about stock. Mel further admitted two of her Brumby mares were in foal, probably due to Carmen's fine stallion covering them on the trip out. Fortunately, they weren't due for a while. Carmen and Fabiola had a good laugh over the burgeoning increases in Mel's stock, glancing at Alinta as she busily and ponderously walked about washing up after dinner. They would have helped, but the aboriginal woman had insisted on doing the dishes and feeding the dogs herself.

"Just as independent as a Yank I know," Carmen whispered, loud enough that Fabiola heard her too, and Mel started to laugh at the dig. Mel had complained good-naturedly how Alinta was becoming more assertive as she learned English.

"She has learned to speak her mind when she knows the words," Mel bragged, proud of the woman and her prowess in the English language.

Carmen smiled for her friend, realizing that she had fallen in love with the pregnant woman. Fabiola was surprised to see that too. She hadn't thought about it herself, and now, knowing that Mel was a woman and not the man she had thought her to be, she realized the relationship that might ensue from this unusual woman. It gave her food for thought.

They only stayed two days while helping to finish building the fold and listening to Mel's plans. Mel sent them on their way, a couple of letters she had written in their possession to be mailed as soon as anyone came to the station. When they left on their way back to civilization, they could take her mail along with the station mail. Mel had told them she intended to buy more sheep, cattle, and horses, and she would also be hiring a couple of stockmen. "But not until next year or maybe the year after next," she insisted, still wanting her peace and quiet.

Mel waved as they left, the empty packsaddles on the extra horses. The two women and a couple of vaqueros who knew her returned the wave. The stockmen nodded, wondering at the odd man who preferred to be all alone in the far Outback with his woman and large flock. They hadn't been privy to the conversations between the women, knowing their place was not with the station owners.

CHAPTER ELEVEN

They were heading out to build their sixth fold when Mel stumbled across a beautiful valley that was hidden among the hills and dips of land that encompassed what she hoped would eventually become her station. The only reason she found the hidden valley was because she was searching for some of her sheep that had broken out of the fold. She didn't know if they escaped because they were due to give birth soon or were just flighty, as some sheep were. While using the dogs to find them, she came across a path she knew was not man-made and followed it. Her horse stepped carefully, and as they crested a hill, which gave her a beautiful view of the Outback, she happened to look over the edge and caught her breath at the sight. The green valley held not only her missing sheep but kangaroos, wallabies, and other animals she didn't recognize. A small waterfall fell from the rocks on one side, and a stream meandered through it, becoming lost on the far side. She realized this might be the very spot she wanted for her home paddock. The valley itself, hidden by the countless hills that led up to it, could be her secure backyard and for her own uses only. The beauty of it alone was something she coveted and wanted to call her own. It was to the east and slightly south of the fifth fold they had built. They had decided they had gone far enough north and were now swinging back.

"Find him sheep?" Alinta asked as she walked laboriously up the hill behind Mel, using her stick to help her.

"Alinta, you shouldn't be walking out here," Mel told her, worrying that she was doing too much again, and it would be bad for the baby that protruded so prominently from her. Mel had seen an arm move across the pregnant woman's stomach last week, and it looked painful.

"Baby strong," Alinta told her, smiling at the other woman's concern. Her adoration for Mel shone in her eyes, but she couldn't seem to make Mel realize that she wanted more. She didn't know how to show her, and she certainly hadn't learned the words she needed to tell the large woman.

Mel got off her horse and held her hand out to the aboriginal woman. When Alinta was standing next to her, she said, "Look at that," pointing to the hidden valley and the sheep grazing in it along with the kangaroos and wallabies.

"Ohh," Alinta breathed out, realizing how beautiful the land was and appreciating it. She'd seen more of the Outback than any of her people, she was sure of it. She was so grateful to have someone to share this with, and soon, she would have a child. She rubbed her stomach and felt a well-aimed kick. She smiled as she looked up at Mel, hoping she would want to raise the child with her. Strangely, she

wished that Mel was the father but understood that wasn't possible. Still, she hoped for so many things and wished she had the words to express herself.

"I think this is where I'll build our home paddock," Mel explained.

"Home?" Alinta asked, unsure of the word.

"Yes, where we will live permanently. The other paddocks will be where the stockmen will take our sheep…like they do at Twin Station." She knew she wasn't explaining it adequately, but she wasn't always sure how much Alinta understood or what words she remembered. Alinta's phenomenal memory made Mel feel ashamed whenever she caught herself talking pidgin English to the woman. The intelligent woman unintentionally reminded Mel to always treat her as an equal. Just because she didn't have the education Mel had didn't mean she wasn't knowledgeable. In fact, Alinta had taught Mel a lot since she had met her. Mel wished she could have more, but she didn't want to take advantage of the pregnant, young woman. The last time she had been involved with a young woman…she immediately squashed all thoughts of Abigail Baxter, now Worthington. Mel had let go of her memories of Abigail on the long ship ride out here. The memories were better in the past.

"You build fold, hut?" Alinta asked.

"Yes, we will build a fold there," she pointed to a spot out of the way of the path that led into the valley. She began squinting as she imagined the house she wanted. The view from the porches would look out into this green and beautiful spot. The sheds and barns she intended to have would be down to the right of the house and out of the way, so they were in no way impeding the view. "We will build sheds, barns, and corrals over there," Mel pointed to another spot as she got excited. "For now, I'll get the sheep," she brought herself back to Earth, knowing she could get excited by her many plans. She sent the dogs down the animal trail after the sheep, who looked up from their grazing when they spotted them. The dogs soon rounded up the sheep and returned them up the path, and Mel sent them back towards the temporary fold they had broken out of.

Mel walked with Alinta back to their camp, not willing to get back on the horse she now led. She enjoyed walking with this woman and wished desperately she could make her feelings known. She also worried if she would be rejected by Alinta, or the woman would be appalled at the suggestion of two women *being* together. There was also the fact that Alinta acquiesced to almost everything Mel wanted to do, which was a product of her upbringing, or so Mel thought. If Alinta gave into everything, would she feel compelled to give in if Mel asked her to be her partner? Would she even understand what Mel was asking? Mel had no way to know that Alinta also had feelings she couldn't make known to the white woman.

Alinta was often too tired to ride the horse all the time, her bulk impeding her ability to climb into the saddle by herself, and she was too uncomfortable when Mel placed her on top of the horse. She loved being close to Mel, and she liked the touches she received from the gentle woman, curiously wanting it more and more as they traveled together, but she had no idea how to make her wishes known.

The next day, they began to build the sixth fold. Mel made this one larger than any of the others she had built, and Alinta helped as best she could, but there was very little she could carry as she trudged back and forth. The rains had stopped, but it was still cold. She waddled, her back hurt, and she could not bend over to pick anything up. Still, she

tried to help as best she could, and she expertly wove wood and plants into the crosspieces that Mel put in place.

They were almost done with this fold weeks later when the sheep began to give birth. Mel showed Alinta what she had to do to help sheep that might be in distress. Alinta tried her best, but she was limited by her girth, and Mel wouldn't let her do too much because of her pregnancy. Alinta was sure she was being overly protective, but at the same time, it felt good that the woman obviously cared. Mel taught her how to listen to a sheep, who made almost no noise as it gave birth, so she could recognize when it did bleat in distress. Alinta brought sheep to Mel's attention time and again, saving them from a horrible death or from the loss of their lambs as the grazer helped to deliver them. Alinta also learned to reach in and help the sheep, the squeezing on her hand painful as she sorted out legs while the acids bit at her skin.

Mel was extremely solicitous to Alinta, concerned for the welfare of her and the baby she was carrying. Alinta began to realize Mel cared for more than just the child, she also cared for Alinta herself. She was hopeful that they could also have more as she knew she cared a lot for the other woman.

It was exhausting work, and the days blended as they helped the sheep to give birth. Mel repeatedly asked Alinta to stop. "Please, just keep me supplied with hot stew and keep me warm," she begged Alinta as she waddled around the large flock looking for sheep to help and leaning on her gathering stick to help her. Alinta did keep her supplied with the large stew they had made, adding wild vegetables she had gathered, which the white woman seemed not to notice. The result was a delicious, hot meal that they both enjoyed as they worked non-stop.

Mel insisted Alinta sleep, but after a few hours, she'd be up helping again. Mel was hard at it as well after even fewer hours of sleep.

Alinta was concerned that Mel slept so little. She herded the sheep to and from the field, but it took so much longer than usual as they were giving birth along the way. Sometimes, she would let the flock go on ahead, the dogs around them, as she stopped to help one of the sheep sort out the many lambs inside that were preventing each other from being born. Alinta brought them both food, so they could keep working. She saw Mel stumbling from sheep to sheep and worried about her. The smell of the afterbirths attracted predators. Not just dingoes were drawn in. Hawks and other birds and animals were also drawn by the odors, and the dogs were busy protecting the flock. One day, Mel's lack of sleep nearly cost her several lambs when the dingoes attacked in a large pack. Mel fired at them with one barrel and then another, and the dogs converged on the predators and fought them off. Frightened at seeing the two pregnant bitches among the throng, Mel pulled at the dogs, earning a snap and a bite from them. Blood was streaming down her hand where she was bitten, but she finally got the bitches away as the rest of the dogs chased away the dingoes. She tied the two bitches up near their hut as Alinta looked on wide-eyed. She quickly helped to bandage Mel's hand as Mel reloaded her gun.

Mel went back to work as soon as she could, but she knew she wouldn't be able to save them all. When she lost sheep and lambs, she skinned the carcasses and put them into bags, cutting up the meat and drying it out with the intention of using it for dog food. She wouldn't eat the dried mutton, but with water added, she thought the dogs might. Alinta could help with that, using the knife she proudly owned and so admired to cut up the carcasses once Mel explained what she wanted

done with them. Mel knew that some grazers would have burned the carcasses, but she didn't want to waste anything, and the dried meat could be stored in the extra empty kegs she had from using up her supplies or even in the bags that went on the packhorses. Rows of drying meat hung around the fire, the smoke keeping flies at bay as Mel continued to help her sheep. Alinta waddled about the forest collecting dried tree limbs to keep the many fires going and dry the meat for Mel.

There were some young lambs whose mamas rejected them because they had too many lambs to care for, and there were one or two lambs whose mamas had died. Alinta watched as Mel tricked some of the mamas who had lost lambs into caring for the rejected lambs, cutting the skin from the dead lambs and putting it on the orphaned lambs. When the orphaned lambs were too fragile, rather than watch them starve to death, Mel butchered them. These were added to the dried dog food supply she had started, and Alinta cut them up willingly for her.

Mel cried from exhaustion, startling Alinta, who had never seen the larger woman cry before. Alinta held Mel tenderly, her arms conveying the deep empathy she was unable to express in words yet. Mel slept in the Aborigine's arms that night as the births tapered off and exhaustion finally took her. She woke up frantic, afraid she had missed some sheep, and she was surprised to find Alinta still holding her. Alinta smiled down at Mel, caressing the side of her face when the Yank looked up, startled. Mel leaned up and placed her lips on the other woman's, then pulled away. Surprised, Alinta touched her lips with her fingertips, wondering at the touch that seemed to tingle. Mel smiled, pulling farther away and getting up to check on her sheep.

"It looks like a good crop," she said proudly as she gazed at the many sheep and their lambs gamboling along beside them. Some were too wobbly to do much more than fall flat on their faces as she let them out to graze. Slowly, the dogs pushed the sheep into the valley, pushing aside the native wildlife as the sheep spread out to munch on the grasses. Their lambs learned to walk and eventually run, becoming stronger with every passing day. Mel glanced at Alinta, who smiled at her shyly, still in wonder over their shared kiss that morning. She brought Mel a plate of food as she watched over her sheep and stayed to watch her eat what she had prepared for her.

Mel showed Alinta how to castrate the males and mulse all the new lambs, cutting a notch in the castrated lambs' ears, so they could identify them as wethers. Alinta understood now that these wethers were for food for them and the dogs. The skin from around the anus, the tail, and the testicles were all thrown into a bucket, and when it was full Mel would throw everything on the fire to burn. The smell of burnt wool was terrible, but the meat smelled good. Mel explained that she didn't want to leave the meat around to attract predators, indicating some of the birds and complaining that they were as bad as dingoes, and they were big enough to carry off a newborn lamb. Alinta watched them closely as she worked, wondering why she didn't feed the testicles to the dogs.

Once this huge chore was done Mel said they had to move to another paddock, so the grass would have time to regrow. Having such a large flock was not a good thing, and the grass had been chewed down. Mel explained that a sheep would eat down to the roots, making it impossible for the grass to regrow. They moved slowly, some delay due to all the lambs and some because Alinta was enormous. Alinta

was miserable on the horse, but she wouldn't let Mel know. She wanted only to help this woman she thought of as her mate. Alinta carried a dog tied up in bags on either side of her saddle. Mel had told her the dogs were carrying pups. They looked as uncomfortable as Alinta felt up there. Mel built their next hut alone since Alinta was too exhausted to help her.

A few days later, Alinta gave birth. She took her cues from her vague memories of what the women of her tribe had talked about, her mother's advice, and what she had witnessed as the sheep gave birth. She barely made a peep when the pains were upon her. Her natural, healthy vitality made it a relatively easy birth, and she effortlessly delivered a daughter. Mel had helped, and she stared wonderingly at this little miracle. Mel wiped the little girl down with a clean cloth and handed her back to Alinta, who looked at her daughter eagerly, examining every feature minutely. Alinta noticed her daughter's skin was lighter than hers. It was not as white as Mel's, but she had the features of a white person. Alinta loved her daughter instantly. She wondered if her own mother had felt this joy upon her birth. She didn't remember her siblings' births well, so she couldn't compare.

Mel burnt the afterbirth in the fire, then went to check on the sheep. She came back to tell Alinta that one of the bitches had given birth at the same time. She gazed on this amazing woman. She was so hearty she might have given birth all alone. Mel's only contribution had been the knotting and cutting of the cord. She watched as Alinta offered her breast to the hungry infant. The sucking began immediately, and she saw the woman cringe slightly when the baby latched on to her engorged nipple. That looked painful to Mel, and she turned to stoke the fire, filling the pot, or billy as it was called, with water and then sprinkling tea in it. Alinta looked down proudly at her healthy daughter, thrilled as she sought and obtained nourishment from her body. As she fed the baby, Mel brought her some tea. It had taken some time for her to get used to the beverage, but the white woman seemed to like it, and it was much different from the coffee they had run out of, which Alinta preferred.

Alinta sleepily watched as Mel left to move the sheep out of the fold. She stopped to talk to the bitch that had given birth. From where Alinta lay she could see the dog wagging its butt as the grazer talked to her, then going back to cleaning her pups. Alinta slept a while to regain her strength, then she woke to feed herself and the baby. She slept again and fed the baby again. The baby didn't seem to feed long, but at least she was getting some nourishment. Something about this little girl stirred all the maternal feelings Alinta hadn't realized she had carried deep inside her. She glanced out to where she knew the sheep were and wondered what Mel might be thinking about her child and what she might be thinking about Alinta. She had feelings for the big woman. She wanted more of that lip on lip, that kiss that Mel had bestowed on her long ago. She'd thought often of it. She wanted Mel to be the baby's other parent. She only wished she could find the English words to make her wishes known to the white woman. After the baby finished feeding, she fell asleep, and Alinta got up to relieve herself, cleaning herself afterward. She now understood that Mel wished her to clean herself, and although water was precious to this woman raised in the desert, and she didn't like how it made her skin feel, she obliged the other woman. She saw where blood had dried on her, and she watched it swirl away in the water as she cleaned up. Alinta quickly hurried back to the hut, not willing to leave the baby

alone too long. She started dinner for Mel and was pleased to see her when she passed by with the sheep that night.

Alinta looked at the woman differently now…from her hat to her broad and blocky face that looked comfortable and kind to the aboriginal woman, to her stocky body that rippled with muscles. Mel had extraordinary strength in that body and had used it to build the folds for the sheep. Alinta admired her greatly. She had also been her teacher and still taught her many things. Alinta retuned the wave and smile as she greeted the grazer.

Over the next two days as they rested at this fold, Mel thought about the long trip south they would soon have to make. According to her calendar—the stick she used to count the days—they should be heading to meet the shearers soon.

Alinta, not understanding what shearer meant, just understood that they would be taking a long journey soon and listened to Mel's concerns.

"Have you decided on a name for your daughter?" she asked Alinta, wondering how much the Aborigine understood each of the English words after so many months together.

Alinta was surprised. She had never thought to name her own child. In her tribe it was the man's right to name his children. She looked at Mel in consternation. "No," she admitted, almost ashamed to admit it. "Mel name daughter?"

"You want me to name your daughter?" she asked to clarify, something she had gotten into the habit of doing long ago to help Alinta with her English.

Alinta nodded, understanding clearly what she was asking.

"I'll think about it. A name is very important." Mel considered, sucking on her pipe. She had not thought of names, and she looked at the child being held in her mother's arms as the mother moved about busily, putting together their dinner and getting the dogs' food ready at the same time. Alinta hadn't needed much time to rest after giving birth. What an amazing woman! Remembering her tutor's Greek philosophy courses, and she thought of the Amazon women, one of which was incarnate standing before her. Primitive perhaps, but just as strong as those warrior women of old.

Alinta nodded again, pleased that Mel would name her child. She looked down at the little girl, amazed that she had given birth to her. Her skin was much lighter than Alinta's, and while she didn't understand all that genetics had given the girl, or who her father really was, she knew that somehow the white man had influenced her daughter's makeup. She didn't quite fully grasp that the rape of her person had caused this little girl, that Bradley's use of her body had impregnated her. Instead, she thought of the first time she had felt the little girl move inside of her and how much Mel had influenced her. She thought of Mel as the baby's other parent, and she believed Mel's influence and presence in Alinta's life caused the baby to be female and to look white.

As Alinta finished feeding the dogs and moved to dish up their food, Mel thought about the name. As she ate, she explained her reasoning to Alinta, not sure how much the simple woman might understand.

"There was an ancient woman in Greece, an Amazon woman, who was the enemy of a great god named Achilles," she told the woman, who listened, not moving as she stared raptly at Mel. Mel took a bite of her food, gesturing with her fork as she spoke. "That woman fought

with a queen named Penthesilea at a place called Troy and against the god, Achilles." She really wondered how much of this story Alinta would comprehend as she didn't have the same understanding about other places, but she wanted to make her understand somehow. "The name Ainia," she pronounced it ah-nee-ah, "means swiftness." Alinta was probably the fastest woman Mel had ever seen before her pregnancy slowed her down. "Your daughter will be named for an Amazon woman, and her name will mean swiftness." She finished her meal and put down the plate, holding out her hands for the baby that Alinta handed her. "Let's name your daughter Ainia, which sounds a little like your name, Alinta but is even more special because she is named after that amazing Amazon woman." Mel looked down at the little girl, seeing that Alinta had cleaned her up completely since the morning when she had given birth. She smiled at the little girl and asked, "Are you, Ainia?"

Alinta didn't understand everything Mel told her, but she did understand that she was naming her daughter after another tribe woman, an Amazon. She liked that the name was like her own, and she understood that her daughter's name meant swiftness. She would constantly ask Mel to repeat the story of the fight between the queen and the god and Ainia's involvement in it. It would become her favorite story, and she felt Mel had chosen correctly, as she had known she would. The white woman knew so many things and didn't mind sharing them with Alinta. She was pleased with the name Mel had given her daughter.

CHAPTER TWELVE

The two women began their long journey back to Twin Station, owned by Fabiola and Carmen. Alinta watched as the sheep—many with twins, triplets, and even some with quads—moved along. She'd heard Mel say that she was so pleased with this crop of offspring that had more than doubled her flock. Alinta wasn't sure what a crop was, but since Mel was pleased, she was happy.

Strapped to the horse Alinta was riding was a bag containing the pups that the bitch wouldn't allow out of her sight. The dog followed the horse constantly and closely, eagerly waiting for the time when they would stop, so the puppies could be let down, and she could nurse them and clean them in her anxiety over their welfare. The other bitch was in a sling on the other side, still hugely pregnant and very unhappy to

be tied to the horse. Alinta wore a wrap that kept Ainia tightly tied to her, so she could easily breastfeed the infant while riding when it was necessary. Behind her were the horses with all their gear piled high and the poles for making the temporary folds were dragging behind them.

The folds they had built so long ago weren't big enough for this large flock, and the temporary fold was also used. Alinta was saddened when the remaining bitch had her puppies and they lost two before Mel could help. Apparently, one large pup had gotten stuck in the birth canal. The rest came out with no problem but not before those first two died.

Alinta worried that Mel wasn't getting enough sleep. She seemed to be up more often on this trip with all the lambs and sheep to watch. She was losing weight, she was short-tempered, and she seemed down. Alinta did what she could to help, taking on more whenever she could by carrying Ainia and working one-handed if she had to.

As they came down off the domed hills, Alinta saw the dust on the horizon long before Mel spotted it. Hours later, Carmen and Fabiola came riding out of the trees with five packhorses behind them and accompanied by only two vaqueros to protect the senora.

"We thought something had happened to you. It's late!" Carmen explained as she took in the enormous flock. "I see you've been busy."

"Busier than I could have ever dreamed," Mel answered, relieved to see her friends. The vaqueros nodded and immediately handed off the packhorses to Alinta before heading to help keep the flock in line.

"You didn't lose any sheep?" Fabiola asked, surprised.

"Oh, yes. We lost plenty. But it's these guys," she indicated the baby, the puppies visible from the sacks on both sides of Alinta's

saddle, and the anxious bitches following at the feet of her horse, "that really made it all worthwhile," she teased.

"Oh, your *baby*," Carmen's voice changed. She sounded like she was crooning as she spoke to Alinta. "What did you have? What did you name it?"

"Baby is girl, and Mel named her Ainia after Greek Amazon and like my name," Alinta told her proudly.

Carmen and Fabiola looked at a blushing Mel in surprise, and then, Carmen smiled. "That's lovely," she told the delighted mother. "I'd like to see her when we stop later. Nothing felt better than holding my babies," she reminisced. "Your English has gotten much better!" she complimented the surprised mother, who smiled shyly.

Mel smiled, enjoying the interaction and feeling relieved to see them. "Have the shearers left?" she worried as she addressed Fabiola.

"No," the Australian shook her head. "We told them we were waiting on some of our farther out flocks and convinced them to stay on. They had a couple of our flocks to do yet, so we should get this flock to them in time. That one was worried about you though," she said, nodding towards a now blushing Carmen.

"You said you'd come in time for the shearers," she accused to hide her embarrassment over her concern for her friend.

"I tried, but this is a lot, and I'll admit…we need help."

"There are a couple men at the station who answered an ad you had someone place for you?" Carmen asked inquiringly.

Mel nodded, relieved. She had more ads she wanted to write, and she would do so in the evenings as they finished the drive. She hoped there was mail for her in addition to the men that had answered the ad.

They discussed the sheep. Mel was happy to see her friend and cousin, and she was hoping to make Fabiola a friend too. She felt the potential was there but understood that the woman hadn't known how to take her before. Now, with nearly a year behind her, Fabiola must understand that there was only friendship between her and her cousin, nothing more.

"Who are the carters?" Mel asked innocently, but both Carmen and Alinta knew the question wasn't as innocent as it seemed.

"Oh, they're the ones I use every year. This will probably be the last year I use them though. Carmen has found some discrepancies in the books and on the invoices over the years."

"Would the name Bradley be among any of the men working for them?" She glanced in time to see Alinta flinch slightly and then looked at Carmen, who was shaking her head to the negative.

"No, I don't recall any of the men being addressed as Bradley. Why? Is there a problem?"

"Well, one of the carters we met on our way out here was named Bradley, and I'll shoot the bugger on sight if he ever comes anywhere near us again," Mel said in a no-nonsense tone and then dropped the subject.

Fabiola looked startled, exchanging a look with Carmen and then looking back at the big grazer and glancing at the gun she wore on her hip as well as the double-barreled musket in her scabbard, both readily at hand. While looking back at Carmen, Mel happened to see the pleased expression on Alinta's face before she looked down at her baby.

"Well, these sheep aren't going to get to your home paddock any faster without our help," Mel stated, walking her horse off in another direction and halting their friendly conversation.

Carmen and Fabiola exchanged another look before they too went to help with the flock. Alinta glanced at the three women and tightened her hold on the reins of the many packhorses she was now holding. She managed to cuddle Ainia closer as she urged her horse on. Mel had been a good teacher, and Alinta was no longer frightened of the strange beast since realizing she was in control of it.

As they turned in to camp, Alinta began to get down from her horse on her own, but Mel was immediately there to help her, smiling shyly at the woman as she caught her. She left to finish setting up her portion of their camp as Alinta turned to take the bags down from her horse and give the pups carried within to the anxious bitches. She put the bags of pups down and out of the way. Returning to where Alinta was setting up their fire and making dinner, Mel stopped to pet the puppies briefly, watching as the bitches cuddled their broods. Both bitches wiggled their butts in greeting, simulating wagging tails that were no longer there.

That night was the first good night's sleep Mel had had in a long time. Knowing that there were others to help watch her sheep, she slept deeply, rising in the early morning to take her own shift. She went into the brush to take care of her business, and upon her return, she heard Ainia fussing and Alinta trying to calm her.

"May I take the baby for you?" she offered and held out her large hands.

Alinta didn't hesitate. She had fed the baby, but she still wouldn't settle down. She watched as Mel talked softly to the infant as she walked off into the early morning light to make her rounds, knowing that just the presence of humans kept some predators away. Alinta rose to go in the brush and do her morning absolutions. She was using water more often now since she learned that Mel liked her clean. She had observed as Mel had washed the baby several times. While Alinta would have rubbed sheep fat on the baby, Mel washed it off. She did allow Alinta to rub the baby with crushed leaves that warded off the constant flies and mosquitos, but then, she also used them once she realized how effective they were. Alinta stoked the fire as the vaqueros sleepily woke and rose.

"Good morning," Carmen whispered as she came up to the warmth of the fire to help.

"Good morning," Alinta replied, understanding the greeting after her months with Mel.

"Where is Ainia?" Carmen asked. She had hoped to cuddle some more with the infant like she had before they went to sleep the previous night. Fabiola too had held the baby, if somewhat awkwardly. She'd compared it to a newborn lamb, causing much hilarity for the other women.

"Mel took her to calm baby," she said inaccurately, almost shyly, as she wasn't used to communicating with anyone but Mel.

Carmen smiled, knowing Mel had been good with her children on the long trek out here. She wondered if the American had wanted children of her own and if that would ever have been a possibility.

Well, if what she suspected between the American and the Australian Aborigine was true, that baby was as much Mel's as it was Alinta's. She busied herself with helping the woman prepare breakfast, so they could all get on their way. It was still a long way across Twin Station.

As they approached the home paddock, other riders rode out to help with the large flock, splitting it into different corrals, so the shearers could start in on the sheep.

Mel and Alinta took one of the empty stockmen's houses, surprised to see a modern house being built on one of the hills beyond the home paddock. "What's that?" Mel asked Carmen as they watched the shearers effortlessly guiding their clippers along a sheep. A good shearer was worth their weight in gold as they quickly and efficiently sheared the sheep. Very little blood was spilled, and the maximum amount of wool was taken from the poor beast, who accepted their lot without any fanfare as they waited patiently to be released. Only occasionally did a sheep fight back, these feisty ones making it interesting for those helping to keep the sheep processed—from pushing them into the chute, to pushing them back into the corrals. Many of the mamas had to seek out their lambs, who had been baahing pitifully while waiting impatiently on their dams after they were separated from them. It still amazed the women and some of the men how quickly a sheep could find its lamb among all that were crying out for their mamas.

"Oh, Carmen didn't like our accommodations," Fabiola said as she came up, hearing Mel asking about the building going on at the hillside. She then went to talk to Mel about the men who had come out to work for her.

One of the men had already been ordered off the station for making trouble down in the Aborigine village by pestering the women. Another had angered Mel when he kept eyeing Alinta, especially when she was breastfeeding Ainia. Not wanting to make a scene or restrict Alinta in any way, Mel had instead glared at the man, her size intimidating him until he stopped his behavior. She wouldn't be hiring him.

Mel was approached by a cleric wanting to baptize the baby, and when he found the large man was not married to the primitive aboriginal woman, he was aghast. He blathered on so long that Mel found herself agreeing to have Ainia baptized.

"How in the world did that happen?" she asked Carmen and Fabiola as they walked along. Fabiola was yelling at the men that were loitering to get back to work.

"He wears you down. He's almost as bad as the priests back in California at the missions. They are forever saving the savages, as they call them."

"Well, I better go explain to Alinta, so he doesn't frighten her. I've also got about a dozen letters to write," she sighed, remembering the pile of letters she had gone through.

"We should be done with your flock tomorrow," Fabiola reminded her, glancing at the men, the sheep they were shearing, and the many carts the men were filling.

"Oh, that means she will be going soon," Carmen said, obviously enjoying their visit and reluctant to see them leave.

"Well, I have a station to establish too," Mel reminded her friend fondly. She'd been thinking of nothing else since they got here, and she watched Fabiola's setup. Already, Carmen's influence was obvious

in the operations of this station and not just in the building of the house on the side of the hill.

Mel forgot to warn Alinta. Instead, she went up the hill to discuss with the builder about the work he was doing for Carmen and the possibility of working for her when he was done.

She returned to the stockmen's house to find Alinta upset.

"Good afternoon, my child. May I speak with you?" said the man of God after he had knocked presumptuously on the door of the house.

Alinta, not used to that noise, had jumped where she was making the bed as Mel had shown her, and she hurried to see who was making the noise. It was an odd man dressed all in black with a white patch under his chin, and he looked at her benignly. She neither nodded or made the gesture with her hand that signified 'no,' but the man opened the screen door and came in once he saw her.

"I understand you have a child?" he asked, seeing the baby lying on blankets on the floor and making sucking noises.

Alinta didn't know if she should be afraid of this man or not. He was not dressed like any other man she had seen among the white men. She just stared at him, waiting.

"We must get her baptized, so she is welcome into the kingdom of our Lord, Jesus Christ," he told her, smiling to show he meant no harm but not sure the simple woman understood him. "Do you know our Lord, Jesus Christ?"

Alinta made a negative motion with her hand, but the white man didn't see it. He saw her simply staring at him, uncomprehending, he thought.

"Our Lord, Jesus Christ can save you and your child!" he told her with the passion of his position. These simple people must be saved! He felt it was his duty to save them all. "We will take the child and pour holy water over its head and baptize it." He smiled again; sure he was being benevolent to the poor child.

Alinta understood many of the words but didn't like their content. She wondered if this Lord Jesus Christ was going to drown her daughter. She bent to pick up the baby and hold her close. Ainia immediately burrowed in, hoping to be fed again, her appetite hearty.

"I've told Mr. Lawrence about it and he has agreed. I'll be happy to perform the ceremony for you. I am a man of God," he told her, pointing to himself, "a religious man. It has also come to my attention that you and Mr. Lawrence are not married. This is a sacrilege! We need to remedy this as well. We could have a double ceremony?" He smiled, unsure if the woman understood him. These were such a simple people.

He had no idea that Alinta did understand what he was saying or that she was of a different tribe than the Aborigines around Twin Station or any others he had met. If Mel agreed to this, Alinta would have to obey. She watched as the man in black left them. She went to the door well after he had left to watch him walking across the yard. She was deeply upset, but Ainia's rootings had produced the desired effect, and her breasts were letting down milk that she must feed to the baby before her cries began.

When Mel returned, she spent a good half hour explaining to Alinta that the ceremony was for religious purposes, not to drown Ainia. "I would never hurt your daughter," she told the woman repeatedly as she attempted to calm her. "This ceremony is so she can enter the kingdom of God," Mel parroted something she had been taught long ago.

"Kingdom?" Alinta asked, confused.

"Remember when we named Ainia?"

The woman nodded, hoping to understand all the words that Mel was telling her. That religious man had used so many words she didn't know.

"I told you of the Greek gods and how Ainia is an Amazon name?"

Alinta nodded, smiling, and said, "An enemy of Achilles?"

"Yes," she answered, pleased with Alinta's memory. "This is about God, the Christian God, and while the baptism won't hurt Ainia, it might help her someday." She was thinking about Ainia growing up, and she realized it would be easier to get along in this English society if she was baptized, even if they were in the Outback and far away from most of the masses. One never knew what the future might hold and how things might change.

"Man say we should marry too," Alinta mentioned. "What be marry?"

Mel suddenly felt very uncomfortable, wondering how to explain the concept of marriage. "It's a ceremony where we would pledge ourselves to each other," she said, watching the woman to see if she understood. "It means you would be my mate for all time, and I would be your mate." Mel wondered if she was being too modest and too simplistic. The ceremony of marriage meant a great deal more to some people.

"Mean Mel no go away ever? Alinta stay always?"

"Do you want to go away? Find your family?" she asked, looking worriedly at her. She had thought her worry that the woman would go with the Aborigines she had seen was long past since she showed no interest in the ones that lived here on the station or the few they had seen in their own wanderings.

Alinta made a signal with her hand. Mel saw it now and knew it meant no. It had taken her a while to learn these signs from the woman, but she watched her body language a lot more now than she had when she had first met the woman. "Family no want Alinta now. Mel, Ainia family now."

"Do you want to marry me?" Mel asked. "Do you want to make it permanent and right in the eyes of the white man?" Her heart was beating frantically right now. She had never considered that she might marry a woman, not even this woman. Men, yes. Long ago she had thought about it, even dreamed about it, but she had realized her fate when she was attracted to women and men didn't want her. She looked in the nearly black eyes of the striking aboriginal woman, hoping she would say yes, yet also afraid she would say yes.

"You want marry Alinta? Become my mate for all time?" Alinta too was nervous. She had no plans to ever leave Mel, but if Mel wanted this ceremony to make it *right* in the eyes of the white man, as she said, then Alinta wanted it too.

"Only if you do," Mel said, but she suddenly felt shy and unsure. "You understand, if they knew what I am…" she began uncertainly. She knew they would never marry her to this woman if they knew that she was female.

"That you are grazer?" Alinta asked, stressing the z sound in a funny way that Mel found endearing.

Mel smiled as she shook her head and addressed the issue she knew Alinta had figured out long ago. Quietly, almost as though someone else was listening, she said, "No. In the white man's world, they do not let women marry other women."

"Why not?" Alinta asked.

Mel shrugged, not willing to debate it with her now. It felt like her heartbeat was going to choke her. It was pounding so hard in her chest it felt like it was working its way into her throat. "That is their way. They do not see the obvious. They do not see that I am a woman and not a man, and they see you as a woman." She looked at the physically fit woman, who was solid and beautiful to Mel. "They think marriage is only between a man and a woman. Do you want a man? A real man?"

Alinta was already shaking her head, knowing Mel didn't always see her hand when she made the sign. "I want Mel," she said simply.

Mel was shaking. "Do you want...?" she was afraid to ask the question. They hadn't gone there but that one time. She was amazed when Alinta made her own wishes known.

"Mel, will you do that lip on lip again?"

Mel turned her head slightly, almost as if she hadn't heard correctly. "You liked that lip on lip?" she parodied and then corrected herself. "It's called kissing."

"Kissing?"

"Yes, when you touch lips it is called kissing. The lip on lip is called a kiss," she explained, feeling foolish.

"Yes, I liked kissing," she admitted, remembering the feeling of closeness and the tingles it had engendered.

"Do you want me to kiss you?" Mel asked, her voice growing huskier as she looked intently at Alinta.

The woman nodded, suddenly feeling shy and not knowing why.

Mel took a hesitant step forward and leaned down to the woman. She desired her so but had been afraid to take it any further. She did not wish to take advantage of the young woman. It hadn't occurred to her that Alinta might want her in return. Gently, she kissed the woman, her lips feeling wonderful beneath Mel's. At first, Alinta just accepted the kiss, but as Mel continued it and softly opened her lips, the woman imitated her, and Mel deepened the kiss, enjoying it when Alinta's hands crept around her body to feel the muscles she had so admired on the fit woman.

Alinta was amazed that a meeting of the mouths could feel so good. Her mother hadn't told her about this when she told her she must accept a man's touch. She had never said anything about accepting a woman's touch. To Alinta, Mel was much more than a woman. She was everything to the aboriginal woman. She was Mel. For her, that was everything, and she eagerly accepted her kisses, realizing as it went on that she wanted more. She was imitating the taller woman and learning. She also realized she wanted Mel's touch and hesitantly put own arms around the large woman, feeling the broad shoulders as she clasped her to her body that was becoming warm.

When Mel reluctantly pulled back because her breathing had increased and she could feel herself becoming very aroused, she stared in Alinta's endless black eyes and nearly fell into them. They were so dark, so mysterious, and so lovely that she couldn't help comparing

them to the endless and vivid night skies she saw here in Australia. She hadn't known her years long wanderings had been leading her to this amazing woman. And she hadn't known that *any* woman would want to spend the rest of her life with her.

"I like kiss," Alinta said softly, her own breathing coming harder. She wondered if the weather was changing as her body was becoming quite warm.

"I do too," Mel admitted, trying to get her equilibrium back. "I think we should wait until the parson marries us to continue this."

"Why?"

"In the white man's world, you only do things like this with your husband or wife, and you only do them after you are married," she explained, wondering briefly at the other women she had been with over the years. They were the reason she had realized she liked the touch of a woman. She realized she wouldn't have known that if she hadn't had sex with them outside the bonds of marriage.

"Then we should do this marry thing," Alinta answered simply. "And the water thing too…for Ainia?" She could hear the baby making waking noises from where she had placed her on the bed after feeding her. She would have to check on her shortly.

"Alinta, I want to marry you. I want to make love to you too. Are you sure this is what you want? You don't want to spend the rest of your life with a man?"

"No. Alinta no want man. Ever. Man hurt me. Man hurt mother. Man no good."

"Not all men are like that," she said, to be fair. Some men were good. Her father had been an excellent example.

"Alinta want no man. Alinta want Mel," she insisted, trying to make herself clear.

Mel smiled brilliantly, leaning down to kiss the woman again. "Mel want Alinta too." She pidginned, wanting her so much it hurt.

CHAPTER THIRTEEN

The marriage of Alinta, a woman of Aborigine descent, to Mel (Melissa) Lawrence from America was performed in the open air of the home paddocks. The sheep were shorn, and the men were packing the bags onto carts to transport them to Sydney. Those in attendance at the wedding were pleased to witness the event. Very few realized the importance of the event or the sex of both the participants.

"Do you, Mel Lawrence…" the cleric droned, having asked for a middle name that Mel did not supply, "take Alinta…" he hesitated over the fact that the woman had no middle or last name. Alinta had given him the name of her tribe, but he couldn't pronounce it, so in his arrogant, white, male way, he just ignored it. He had gotten what he wanted, marriage between these two sinners. It was obvious they had been fornicating; the result of their sins was the child that the woman was holding in her arms. He had no idea that the child was not biologically Mel's, nor did he know Mel was a woman. Only four people there knew Mel's sex, and they weren't telling. The cleric continued, "to be your lawfully wedded wife? To have and to hold from this day forward? For better, for worse, for richer, for poorer? In sickness and in health? To love, cherish, and honor above all others, till death do you part, according to God's holy law?"

"I do," Mel said clearly, her throat closing off as the importance of the words penetrated. She was holding Alinta's hands firmly, looking down at the woman earnestly. They were both dressed nicely. Mel had pulled out one of her suits, which was now tighter in the shoulders and looser around the middle. Alinta's eyes had widened at the sight of her mate in the unfamiliar clothing. Mel had given Alinta her only dress, which she then pinned in for the occasion since it swam on the shorter woman, but it looked like a summery gown with the extra folds causing it to bloom at the waist and making it look attractive on the Aborigine.

"Do you, Alinta take Mel Lawrence to be your lawfully wedded husband? To have and to hold from this day forward? For better, for worse, for richer, for poorer? In sickness and in health? To love, cherish, and obey till death do you part, according to God's holy law?"

Alinta had been ready to say yes. She had been nodding after each thing the man said, and she had understood all the words, but he hadn't stopped, he just kept adding to them. Only the fact that Mel had agreed to almost all the same words had her answering in a small, clear voice, "Yes."

"You are supposed to say, I do," he told her condescendingly. He didn't see Mel stiffen at the tone in his voice but Alinta did, and she quickly said, "I do." She didn't know why Mel was suddenly angry.

Maybe she was mad at Alinta for not knowing the right way to respond? But Mel was now smiling down at her brilliantly as the man continued his nonsense words and finally proclaimed that they were, "Man and wife." Then, he gave Mel permission to kiss her. Alinta blushed as the white woman leaned down and gave her a peck on the mouth in front of all the witnesses, many whistling and clapping.

"I wonder how long until Alinta doesn't obey Mel," Carmen whispered to Fabiola, who was hard pressed not to laugh about the independent woman.

Their wedding was immediately followed by the baptism of Ainia, who was given a second and third name.

"I baptize thee, Ainia Mary Lawrence," the clergyman said, pleased that he could perform this small ceremony for them. He had blessed the water, so it was holy, and he poured the water on the child's head. He was expecting her to cry, but instead, to the amazement of those watching, the child giggled. Mel laughed and Alinta smiled. The clergyman was horrified. He had never heard of such a thing. The crying was supposed to signify the bad spirits and the devil leaving a purified child's body, but instead, this child laughed. He stared in horror at this child of mixed races.

Carmen, one of the godparents, looked on amused when Ainia giggled instead of crying. Jose, the other godparent, looked startled but seeing the senora's amusement, Mel's laughter, and Alinta's smile, he grinned.

As Mel and Alinta turned away from each other to accept congratulations from those attending, Alinta was surprised to be embraced by the women and kissed on the lips by the men. She didn't

like that and would have bolted but for Mel's hand firmly holding her own and Ainia being held in her arms.

Mel saw the Aborigines from the small village watching, some knowingly, and she nodded towards them respectfully, especially the elders, who returned her nod of respect. She had spoken to a few of the elders who spoke English, and she told them they would be welcome at her station, if they so desired. She would need workers, and if they knew of others, they should come see the station she was going to build.

Mel couldn't believe how much the documents filled out by the clergyman meant to her. Seeing her name on the marriage certificate meant as much to her as the baptismal certificate. For better or worse, Alinta was her wife, and Ainia was her daughter. She valued one as much as the other. She rolled the papers up carefully, tying them with a ribbon and planning to tuck them away with her other important papers later.

"Well, you did it," Carmen said knowingly, leaning up to pull Mel down for a kiss on the cheek. "I hope you will both be very happy.

"I hope we will be happy too. Thank you," she told her friend.

Fabiola wasn't quite so friendly, but she also told the large woman she hoped she would be happy. "I'm glad you decided on that land north of us. If I had known about your valley, maybe I would have expanded up there, although that would certainly be a huge station. But I'd rather have a friend there." She held out her hand to shake Mel's, and the American took it gladly. She wondered briefly if Ainia would grow up to be as beautiful as this woman of mixed races, and she looked at the woman speculatively, wondering about her as she glanced between Carmen and the station owner.

Harold was next, having returned after helping one of the stockmen get his shorn sheep out to new pasturage and checking some of the southern paddocks they were hoping to reuse. He heartily congratulated Mel but moved on quickly, not acknowledging Alinta, and Mel noted that. He moved determinedly to the table where some of the stockmen's wives had set up some rum in a keg along with some food for their little celebration. The men packing up the bags of wool rotated out, so they could get a share of rum and a little food before they had to be going. The carters were anxious to be on their way knowing how long a trek it would be back to Sydney.

That evening, Mel handed the lead carter a bag with mail that could be sent out from Wilcannia or Menindee, depending on which place the man decided to travel through. The men were leaving early the next day, and a mail carrier would take it from there. That would be much faster than the carter could take it since it would take months for him to make his way back to Sydney with his full carts of wool. There was much more wool than he had anticipated, and he hadn't had a chance to discuss next year's cartage with the station owner. He had no idea that Fabiola and Carmen didn't intend to use his services next year or that some of the mail he carried contained inquiries to other drayage companies for both Twin Station and the newly formed Lawrence Station.

Mel had spent the afternoon after her wedding going through the large pile of mail from her lawyer, her accountant, a Mrs. Waters, her business partner, and surprisingly, a letter from Abigail in England. Abigail had written Mel soon after arriving in Sydney, wanting to let her and other people she stayed in contact with know of her new *home* and where to reach her. There were also a few other letters, and she spent time answering them all and writing quite a few new letters. Mel wasn't sure how to address the fact that she had married a woman with her lawyer here in Australia and thought it best that she *think* about that for a while. She did, however, make Alinta and Ainia Lawrence her heirs, writing to her father's lawyers—now hers—in America and England. For all anyone else knew, she might have adopted them. It would take time for the letter to reach the Americas and England, so she had some breathing room.

"What is that?" Alinta asked as she nursed Ainia, the dress she had enjoyed long gone, replaced by her clean man's long shirt and miners' pants, her feet once again bare.

"This is writing," Mel explained as she finished up one letter, addressed it, and sealed it.

"What is writing?" the inquisitive and always interested woman asked.

Mel realized her wife—she loved the sound of that—had never seen her read or write. That gave her another thought, and she decided to write the lawyer and request some books be sent to her. Thinking about that further, she knew she wanted the classics but perhaps, some basic books would be good to teach her wife and someday, her daughter, how to read and write. "This is how we communicate across long distances. This is from America, the land where I come from," she said, pointing to the letter she had just answered from her lawyers there. "That one is from England, from a friend of mine that lives there." She had written Abigail too, knowing it might be a year before she heard from her again. Still, ships went to England and the Americas all the time. It was the mail service from Sydney to the interior that would really take a lot of time. She'd explained to all

involved how far out her station was that she was establishing and that was why it was so long between letters.

"You teach Alinta?"

"Sure, I'll be happy to teach you," Mel replied, having just had that thought. "We will teach Ainia too someday." Mel was so happy. She had a companion and a daughter, perhaps for the rest of her life. She was a realist. She wanted to believe everything was forever, but they lived so far away from everything, and things could happen.

Alinta was happy too. She didn't know what the future held, but with Mel as her mate, she was looking forward to finding out. She looked down at her daughter and held her tighter knowing that they were safe with this woman-man and secure in the knowledge that Mel wanted them with her forever. She looked down at the odd little ring that someone had sold Mel. It had come from one of the stockmen, who had lost the woman he planned to marry. She thought it an odd custom to wear such metal, but once she got used to seeing it on her left hand, she also thought it pretty. Mel had explained the ring was worn on that finger because white men thought it went directly to their heart. She said it with a sweet smile on her face as she explained, and Alinta's heart was happy too.

~THE END~

About the Author

K'Anne Meinel is the BEST-SELLING author of LAWYERED, REPRESENTED, SAPPHIC SURFER, DOCTORED, VEIL OF SILENCE, SURVIVORS, VETTED and CAVALCADE as well as several other books including her first, SHIPS which was written in 2003 over the course of two weeks. A gypsy at heart, she has lived in many locations and plans to continue roaming. Videos of several of her books are available on YouTube outlining some of the locations of her books and telling a little bit more…giving the readers insight into her mind as she created these wonderful stories. As of this date she has more than 102 published works including shorts, novellas, and novels. She is an American author born in Milwaukee, Wisconsin and raised in Oconomowoc. Upon early graduation from high school she went to a private college in Milwaukee and then moved to California for seventeen years before returning to the state. Many of her stories have Wisconsin in them as settings for her wonderful, realistic, and detailed backgrounds. Named the lesbian Danielle Steel of her time, K'Anne continues to write interesting stories in a variety of genres in both the lesbian and mainstream fiction categories. Her website is www.kannemeinel.com.

If you have enjoyed **OUTBACK BORN**, I hope you will enjoy this excerpt from
CAVALCADE

Molly didn't know what kind of life to expect when she fell in love with Erin Herriot—her schoolmate, her best friend, and a woman. She had been grateful for Erin's friendship when the bank swindled her after selling her parents' farm and she was invited to live on Erin's parents' farm.

After making the difficult decision to live life as 'man and wife,' Molly gladly accepted the challenges before them. Together, they made the decision to sell Erin's farm and embark on the journey of a lifetime...on the Oregon Trail.

Erin couldn't give Molly children; however, she could love her forever. But leaving the area where they had both grown up and where everyone knew the women was the only way they could be together without questions about the true nature of their relationship.

Come along on their adventure as two women cross the country, adopt a family, and begin a life that neither had imagined possible growing up in the mid-1800s.

CHAPTER ONE

Erin watched as Molly labored over the dog, petting her to calm her frantic breathing. Both Erin and the male dog watched for hours as one by one, the woman helped the first-time mother bring forth her litter of puppies. Two of the barn cats looked on curiously from the hayloft

above the stall. The time sped by, but no one left their post. Erin shifted from foot to foot occasionally, looking down at the male Tervuren, who looked up in excited wonderment, panting happily. The intelligence of the Belgian dog showed through in that look they exchanged.

"Well, I think she's done. That's it, eight pups," Molly finally said as she palpated the abdomen. She smiled down at the bitch, who nuzzled at the tiny, mewling creatures. She seemed confused about what they were and the fact they had emerged from her body. Her flightiness was now gone, soothed by Molly's comforting presence. Already, she had licked each of her offspring thoroughly and allowed this human to examine them. She lay contentedly now as they finished their first feeding, nuzzling close to the warmth of the fur around her teats.

"That's a good litter for her first," Erin commented with a smile, leaning down to pet King, who looked up at her again as though he understood. "Think we can let him near her?" she indicated the proud papa, who had watched the birth of each of his pups, cocking his head now and then at the noises emanating from them.

"She'll let him know if she doesn't want him near," Molly said as she rose from her kneeling position, stretching her back after being scrunched over for so long. The front of her apron was covered with slime from the puppies she had helped whelp.

"Do you really think she needed your help?"

"Ya, I think she was frantic until I settled her here." She indicated the stall they had prepared for the whelping box.

Erin had to concede that Molly was probably right. For a first-time mother, Queenie had been rather ditzy, so unlike the normal brilliance they experienced in Tervurens. Erin knew this relatively unknown breed was invaluable here on the farm and was worth the effort. She gazed at the exhausted bitch. This part of her job was mostly over, and she was laying back in the deep straw, her smooth and even breathing indicating she was asleep.

Molly backed up farther, slowly, so she could look down at the display. King chose that moment to take hesitant steps into the stall, sniffing avidly. Queenie never woke, didn't give any indication she even knew her mate was there. Both humans tensed, ready to pull the male away if he gave any indication that he would savage the pups. Instead, he sniffed each one individually and nudged it slightly with his nose, familiarizing himself with each of the eight pups before he turned his back and lay down, protecting his mate and family and looking at his humans. His expression clearly indicated they could go. He had this. He wouldn't let anything happen to his family.

Molly smiled as she took one lantern hanging on the stall. Erin took the other lantern as they left the animals, closing the barn door behind them.

"I am tired," Molly admitted as she stretched again, the fabric of her dress pulling tightly against her form, showing her firm, young breasts and drawing Erin's eyes.

"You should be. She was at it a long time."

"I just worried that she would step on one. I've never seen a dog go from sensible to scatterbrained so quickly."

"I'm sure I'd have been just the same," Erin admitted with a laugh. They shared a laugh as both knew Erin would likely never have children. At the same time, it saddened them, but neither spoke that aloud as they headed for the farmhouse.

"We better get some sleep before I have to get up for chores," Erin mentioned as she put her lantern on the counter.

"And I better set this in cold water to soak," Molly mentioned, removing her apron.

Erin worked the handle of the pump in the sink, and Molly put a pan beneath it to catch the splashing water. They worked harmoniously and silently together. They were a well-organized team, each confident the other would do their part and be there for the other.

"This gunk soaked right through. I'm going to have to bathe," Molly lamented, surveying the mess on her apron.

Erin pumped the handle, filling pans of water and setting them on the stove to warm for a bath for Molly. She didn't mind helping, and they soon had the bathtub ready. As Molly stripped, seeing her in the lantern light, arching into the towel, set Erin's teeth on edge. She was so beautiful, and her dark good looks enticed the woman. Erin was breathless watching Molly, who was unaware how alluring she looked with the towel wrapped around her, her dark reddish-brown hair, and her sultry, dark eyes that perpetually looked as though they were made up with cosmetics but were all natural. She quickly turned to clean up the kitchen as Molly let out the bathwater.

Only when everything was set up in the kitchen, did Erin blow out the two lanterns and take a candle she had lit. They headed to their

bedroom, passing the stairs that led upstairs to the other four bedrooms in the old farmhouse.

"Do you think we'll ever fill those?" Molly asked, glancing at the door and then realizing she had spoken aloud. "I'm sorry," she quickly added as she hurried to get ready for bed. It was late, and she was sorely tired.

"Anytime you want to go to the orphanage down in Melville, you let me know," Erin told her.

"But the deception of it all," she exclaimed worriedly. She went to pull on her nightgown.

"What deception? They will think, like others do, that I'm a man. I just need to spell my name A-a-r-o-n instead of E-r-i-n is all. Although, maybe that isn't necessary. There are men named Erin."

"I don't think God would like that kind of lying," she said primly. She quickly pulled the curtains on the bedroom windows, even though they were far out in the country and no one could see them.

"I don't think God puts people on Earth to lose their parents either. We can give a child a good home, maybe even two children. If we are gonna live according to the Bible, we must help our fellow man."

"Well, I'm sure God didn't put you in my path none either," Molly answered pertly.

Erin was removing her boots, her overalls, and her shirt as they had their familiar conversation. They'd had this conversation a few times since they started living together and sleeping together as though they were man and wife. As far as their neighbors knew, they were two women helping each other out. No one needed to know they were

intimately acquainted. The house was big and there were beds made upstairs to indicate that one of them lived up there, if anyone cared to look. "You want me to sleep upstairs?" she teased.

"Not unless I'm mad at ya," Molly teased in return, her face softening. She wouldn't have thought she'd fall in love with a woman but she had. After the death of her folks, the bank's subsequent sale of their farm, and the pitiful amount she was compensated, she had nowhere to go. Her best friend from school, Erin, had offered her a place.

"You mad at me?" Erin asked, checking to be sure. Down to her drawers, she couldn't hide the small bumps on her chest that she kept wrapped up. They weren't much, but the wrapping made them seem more like a muscular man than a woman with breasts. Only people who knew them, people who had grown up around Stouten and knew her family, knew she was a woman. Strangers were always fooled.

"Whatever for?" Molly asked, putting her arms around Erin and hugging her close.

"I don't know. You gals are always thinkin' up somethin'," she answered, leaning into the hug and relishing it. She could smell how fresh Molly was from her bath, and she remembered how good she had looked in the lantern light. She never thought she'd have anyone in her life. She hadn't thought a woman would take her on, and she knew she didn't want a man, although some men wanted her for the fine farm her father and brothers had left her to tend. Had her parents or brothers still been alive, she was certain she'd have been married off to some man who didn't mind the fact that she looked every bit as masculine as him.

Her hair being pinned back in a bun was the only clue that she was a woman.

"Nope. I'm pleased with ya right now, real pleased. We got us a fine litter of Tervurens that should fetch as much as two bits each if we are careful who we sell 'em to."

"That sounds like too much," she lamented, but she too was hoping to get as much as that for the Tervurens. According to Erin, not many people knew of the breed. She'd found Queenie last year at a farmers' market. She was a skittish thing without many prospects, so she'd gotten her in trade for two chickens. King had been happy with her choice; he finally had a playmate. He didn't realize until she came into season that she was to be his mate. Erin hadn't let him mate her that first time; Queenie was just too young. Her second season, he'd gotten his chance and done a fine job of getting her with pups…a fine job.

"Well, it all counts…every *extra* cent," she reminded her of their plans.

"Yep, it shore does," she agreed as they got into bed together.

They were saving every dime they could squeeze from the farm. They had taken the pitiful sum that Molly had gotten after the bank took their share from the sale of her parents' farm and added it to Erin's savings. They'd told no one of their plans. People wouldn't have permitted such plans. Two women alone on a farm was bad enough, and there were already a few bachelors determined to change that. Most were interested in Molly, but every now and then, a man was determined to win Erin over. Their desire wasn't for the woman but for the family farm. It was an established farm, one that didn't require

constant expansion and was worth a lot of money. Her brothers, father, and uncles had all worked themselves to death clearing the land for her grandfather, who had settled here. If they had survived, they would have been proud of the work Erin put in to keep it going. Well, maybe not. She wasn't in her 'proper' place as a woman. She didn't mind, but many men would, including those in her family. Right now, she couldn't worry about that; she was the only one who had survived.

They cuddled close, pleased with themselves and the results of their breeding of the two dogs. "When do you think we can go?" Molly asked, knowing a lot hinged on their money situation.

"I'm hoping next spring. Let's see what the harvest brings this year, and we'll see what other money we can find."

They'd been saving for two years, ever since Molly had agreed to live with Erin. They knew they couldn't stay in this area where everyone knew them and where they had grown up. Already, there were some suspicions being cast their way, especially since Molly had already turned down two offers of marriage. Erin's only offer had been for her farm, but they had generously offered to 'allow' her to stay on it, with him. It was understandable that she turned him down, but it didn't mean there weren't others who would be willing to take her on despite her masculine appearance. But no one was going allow the two women to remain *spinsters*, not when a fine farm and an attractive woman like Molly were in the equation. Somehow, someway, someone would try to change that; they were already trying.

"Then, next spring, we'll go to Melville. No point feedin' any young'uns over the winter when we're tryin' to save."

"That's true," Erin admitted. She knew she would never be able to give Molly a child of her own body. She had offered to bow out and let Molly marry one of the men who had come courting as they could give her the child she wanted so much. They didn't love her though; they simply wanted a wife. Molly wanted love, something her parents hadn't had. Molly loved Erin and knew her best friend loved her too. To find out that there was physical pleasure in each other's arms too had been a bonus. She wanted a life with Erin, a forever life.

They were both tired. The bitch had gone into labor late in their normal workday, and the hours spent calming her and watching her give birth had made them miss their supper. It was too late to eat anything, so they both went to sleep on empty stomachs. It wasn't the first time, and it certainly wouldn't be the last.

~End sample chapter of CAVALCADE~

For more go to www.Shadoepublishing.com to purchase

the complete book or for many other delightful offerings

 *~ Because a publisher should stand behind their authors~*

 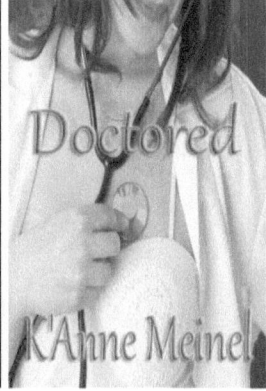 

www.shadoepublishing.com

~ Because a publisher should stand behind their authors~

What do you do when you meet someone who changes everything you know about love and passion?

Paige Harlow is a good girl. She's always known where she was going in life: top grades, an ivy league school, a medical degree, regular church attendance, and a happy marriage to a man. Falling in love with her gorgeous roommate and best friend Alyssa Torres is no small crisis. Alyssa is chasing demons of her own, a medical condition that makes her an outcast and a family dysfunctional to the point of disintegration make her a questionable choice for any stable relationship. But Paige's heart is no longer her own. She must now battle the prejudices of her family, friends, and church and come to peace with her new sexuality before she can hope to win the affections of the woman of her dreams. But will love be enough?

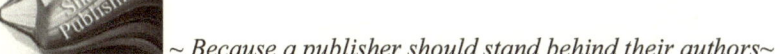

~ Because a publisher should stand behind their authors~

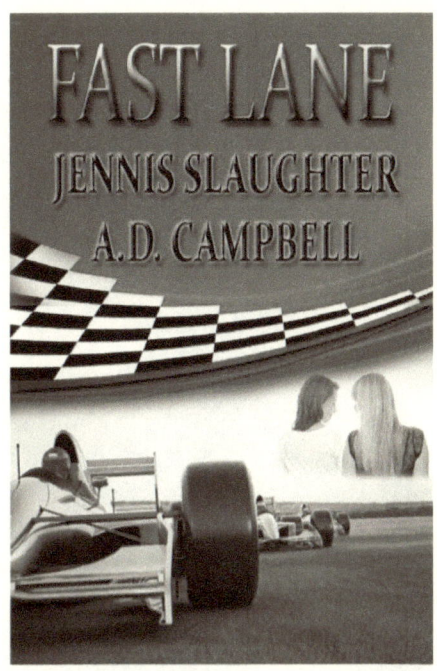

In the male dominated sport of Formula 1 racing, Samantha 'Sam' Dupree is struggling to make her mark against the boys. She hears about a driver who is making a name for herself in NASCAR and goes to check her out. Little does she know that she's in for the race of her heart.

Addison McCloud wants nothing more than to drive. She doesn't care about fame or fortune; she just wants to be fast enough to get herself and her family away from her abusive father. Meeting Sam, changes her world and revs her life into overdrive.

When the two women meet, sparks flies like the race cars that they drive. Will they be able to steer their relationship into something more and win the race, or will their families make them crash and burn. The boys of Formula 1 are going to learn that Southern girls are a force to be reckoned with.

www.shadoepublishing.com

~ Because a publisher should stand behind their authors~

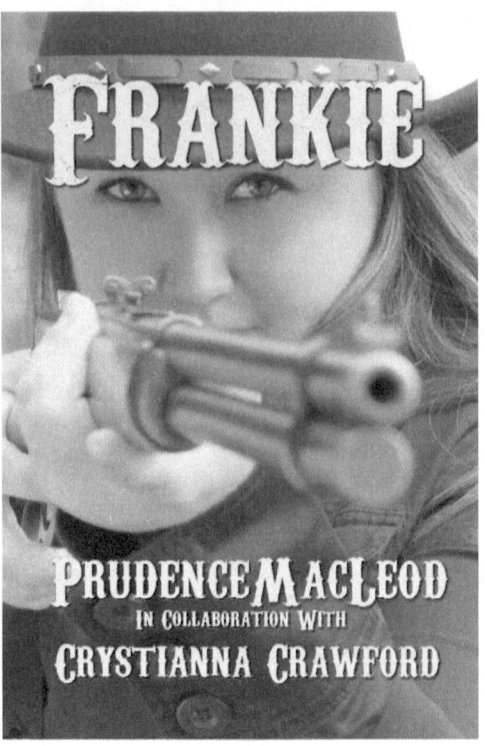

Carrie flees from the demons of her present, trying to protect the ones she loves.

Frankie hides from the demons of her past, and the memory of loved ones she failed to protect.

A modern day princess thrown to the wolves, Carrie's only hope is the rancher who had spent the better part of a decade in self imposed, near total, isolation. Frankie's history of losing those she tries to save haunts her, but this madman threatens her home, her livestock, her sanctuary. She knows she can't do it alone, has she still got enough support from her oldest friends?

www.shadoepublishing.com

 *~ Because a publisher should stand behind their authors~*

Amelia Gittens had the credit of being the first and only woman thus far in the United States military of being a sniper in combat, made possible by being in the Military Police unit of the crack 10th Mountain Infantry Division. After retirement she joins the City of New York Police Department, and suddenly finds herself involved in a suspect shooting incident which soon encroaches upon her entire life. In order to protect her therapist who has been targeted as a revenge killing, Amelia takes on the responsibility as if she was still in the Army, treating it as a tactical maneuver.

www.shadoepublishing.com

~ Because a publisher should stand behind their authors~

When U.S. Marine Dakota McKnight returned home from her third tour in Operation Iraqi Freedom, she carried more baggage than the gear and dress blues she had deployed with. A vicious rocket-propelled grenade attack on her base left her best friend dead and Dakota physically and emotionally wounded. The marine who once carried herself with purpose and confidence, has returned broken and haunted by the horrors of war. When she returns to the civilian world, life is not easy, but with the help of her therapist, Janie, she is barely managing to hold her life together...then she meets Beth.

Beth Kendrick is an American history college professor. She is as straight-laced as they come, until Dakota enters her life, that is. Will her children understand what she is going through? Will she take a chance on the broken marine or decide to wait for the perfect someone to come along?

Time is on your side, they say, unless there is a dark, sinister evil at work. Is their love strong enough to hold these two people together? Will the love of a good woman help Dakota find the path to recovery? Or is she doomed to a life of inner turmoil and destruction that knows no end?

www.shadoepublishing.com

If you have enjoyed this book and the others listed here Shadoe Publishing, LLC is always looking for first, second, or third time authors. Please check out our website @ www.shadoepublishing.com For information or to contact us @ shadoepublishing@gmail.com.

We may be able to help you bring your dreams of becoming a published author to life.

www.ingramcontent.com/pod-product-compliance
Lightning Source LLC
Chambersburg PA
CBHW020246150626
46552CB00020B/478